ARCHITEUTHIS

A CREATURE FEATURE BY MICHAEL COLE

ARCHITEUTHIS

WWW.SEVEREDPRESS.COM

ISBN: 978-1-923165-85-4

CHAPTER 1

"Is this him?"

Jaas kept his AK-47 pointed low as he hurried across the sandy beach to his partner's position. Sanun, a tall pirate with a red bandanna on his head and a sleeveless blue shirt exposing lean, but defined arms, stood at the wreckage at what had once been a thirty-foot dock.

For the entirety of the three years they had been occupying this island, that dock had served them faithfully. Here on Rook, they cooked their product and smuggled it out, all the while bringing in the necessary ingredients from their boss' business associates. Tonight, it was nothing more than a series of broken planks, slowly being claimed by the surf.

In the center of the scattered debris was a single arm, fingers half-coiled, their tips burrowing into the sand as though it was still attempting to crawl to safety. It was all that remained of Ruang Sak, the pirate assigned to lookout at this dock, for behind the shoulder was a few strands of flesh and a slab of jagged bone.

No matter how well things went, the boss never let his guard down. Twenty-four-seven, somebody was on watch. It was the military training that was ingrained in the guy after three years of service in the Royal Thai Armed Forces. If an unidentified vessel was on approach, it could possibly mean trouble.

Jaas swallowed. He had seen and done plenty of horrible things. It was the nature of the trade. But something about seeing his own pal having been butchered nearly resulted in a nasty gag reflex. And there was no doubt that arm belonged to his buddy Ruang Sak. The tattoo of a knife on the wrist was the tell.

"Nobody's heard anything?" he asked Sanun.

The tall pirate shook his head and wiped his sweaty face with a rag.

Standing behind him was Faadil, a bearded pirate who ate more than his fair share of American chocolate bars. Most people claimed that drugs such as the heroin the pirate gang produced was poisoning the world. As far as Jaas was concerned, it was excessive amounts of sugar. More people died from that than their product.

"Maybe it was that one vessel we saw earlier," Faadil said.

"The white yacht with the woman?" Sanun said. He shook his head and lit his fourth cigarette in a row. "I don't think so. We've been quietly keeping tabs on them. According to the boss, they're American researchers. Sea animal stuff."

"How do we know they're not with some agency?" Faadil asked. "An unassuming person is exactly who'd I'd send if I was trying to figure out the whereabouts of a major drug operation."

"There's three people aboard the boat," Sanun said. "One is a woman, one's a kid, and the man is not exactly someone I would consider an adequate security detail. They wouldn't send a group like that after people like us for more than a couple of hours."

Jaas nodded in agreement. The reputation of pirates was an accurate one indeed, and it extended throughout the centuries, no matter what part of the globe they roamed. When he saw the blond on that yacht, he had some unsavory thoughts of his own. It wasn't often he got to see a golden-haired woman in that athletic form. Had it been any ordinary day cruising the ocean, he would probably oblige himself some pleasure with an unwilling participant. For him and the others in their group, the unwillingness was what made it so exciting.

But this group did not want to bring any unwanted attention to themselves. This was a job that brought a lot of money, and it did not require pillaging unsuspecting boaters. Soon enough, he would get back to the fun of hijacking ships and terrorizing their crew. For now, he was a simple soldier tasked with guarding this precious island.

"Have any of the other posts reported anything suspicious?" Jaas asked Sanun.

"No," Sanun replied, halfway through his smoke. "Just these two docks wrecked for no reason. On that note, I have yet to check in with Paari." He dug out his crummy radio from his back pocket and brought it to his lips. "Paari, report in." He lowered it and waited for a response that never came. Frustrated, he tried again. "Paari, get your thumb out of your ass and report."

Again, no response came.

Jaas took a turn. "Paari, if you're asleep when we get over there, we're kicking your ass."

With that said, the three men quickly headed west in the direction of Paari's post. Lit only by the stars and a half moon, they moved along the beach, taking in the sounds of surf rolling up to their feet. All the while, they remained wary of any potential intruders.

The main camp was well-guarded, even though there was a shortage of pirates at the moment. Not until Jimmu returned with his shipment would they be back to full force.

They crossed two hundred yards of sand and trees until they came to the small beachfront wooden shack where Paari was located. Beachfront was too kind a term, as the sand had ended fifty paces back, and was now nothing but rocks, dirt, and some vegetation growing along the shoreline. The small building itself was only a few yards from the waterline.

The patrol came to a stop. Even in this low visibility, the change in the shack's form was unmistakable. It did not stand in its usual cube shape, as it was uprooted by a tremendous force and spread across the shoreline. Like the dock, it was in pieces.

Now, all three men had their AK-47s pointed.

"We were here an hour ago," Sanun said. "Everything was fine."

"Someone's got to be here," Faadil said. "Maybe a naval unit, or some agency task force."

Jaas shook his head. "That doesn't make sense. If someone wanted to infiltrate our camp, why bulldoze through the guard posts? They'd want to take out sentries quietly and not attract attention."

"And what the hell did they use?" Sanun said. He moved to the edge of the wreckage and tapped one of the wooden planks with his foot. "This wasn't demolition. And there's no tracks or any other sign of some sort of vehicle." His gaze went to the pieces that were floating in the water. "Unless…"

"A boat?" Faadil suggested.

Sanun turned his weapon to the open ocean and slowly took a few steps into the water. He searched for anything unusual in the surf; any rigid shapes that would indicate a vessel.

Fed up, he grabbed a flashlight and beamed it into the water. He found floating pieces of wood, rolling waves approaching shore… and a loose strand of fabric that was once Paari's vest.

Jaas saw it too.

The guard had been pulled out to sea and utterly annihilated. If the shredded clothes were not enough for him to figure that out, the floating shoe with the bloody stub of a foot protruding out of it certainly was.

"What the…"

Sanun turned around. "Let's get back to—"

The ocean came alive with an explosion of water cresting over the shoreline and those standing on it. Through the veil of breaking water and the sounds of chaos that came with it, Jaas saw the serpentine forms extend in their direction.

In the blink of an eye, Sanun was no longer there. Only a confused and panicked shriek allowed his comrades to know his destination.

The pirate was pulled thirty feet offshore, caught in the grasp of the blood-red limb that constricted him like a boa. There was a sound of crackling bones and grunts that descended into gurgling sounds as blood came up through his mouth.

A moment later, he was pulled beneath the waves.

As the pirate met his final fate, the horror continued for his onlookers. More limbs, each one permeating the air with a foul odor, stretched from the water to the shoreline. They moved with murderous intent, each one having the length to snatch the stunned men on land.

Faadil tried to back away, but was seized by the leg. The thing, lined with suction cups on its underside, pulled him into the water. The pirate fell on his back and rolled to his belly, screaming as he dug his fingers in the space between the rocks.

Another narrow fiend arose, its end widening like the club of a medieval weapon. Except, it was not rigid, but made of the same muscly flesh that comprised the rest of the limb.

And there was no doubt these were limbs, all attached to a colossal body. Their features, while larger than any other example Jaas had ever seen, were still easily identifiable to any seafaring man.

Tentacles.

The one with the club came down hard and pried the screaming pirate from his grasp. It did so with brute force… removing his arm from the shoulder.

Trailing blood, Faadil disappeared into the swashing surf.

Jaas let loose a spray of bullets. There was no attempt for proper aim or precision. He simply hoped that the reputation of the AK-47 would live up to its potential and take down the army of arms in one fell swoop.

The beast had no fear of the weapon. Any hits that penetrated its tentacles either went unnoticed, or were so insignificant they were not worth retreating from, like a needle prick to a man.

Jaas felt the crushing force of one of the arms as it looped around him. Intense pain filled his body. There was more than pressure, but the slicing of skin and muscle tissue. From those suckers came some sort of razor-sharp accessory, like fishhooks, designed for securing victims. As if the strength of the constriction wasn't enough.

Maybe the beast just liked to inflict pain.

Jaas was yanked off the shore and carried into the water. Next thing he knew, he was submerged.

The glow of Sanun's dropped flashlight twirled under the waves, its glow sweeping over the head and body of the intruder. Jaas saw the umbrella of flesh where the limbs connected with the head.

From the middle of the group extended a massive beak, shaped like an eagle's. From between them came a long, narrow tongue lined with three columns of razor-sharp teeth.

It was here that Jaas would truly know pain. It would be the last thing he would ever know.

CHAPTER 2

"Jon… Jon… Hey! Jon!"

He awoke with a shake, ripped from a pleasant dream where he was going into the movie theater with his father. It was both a memory and a fantasy, not just the setting, but the person he was sharing it with.

His feet were dangling over the side of the bunk, the socks wearing away with big holes in their bottoms.

Standing at the door of his stateroom was his mother, Tracie Otrin. *Doctor* Tracie Otrin, as most people referred to her.

Jon felt sick every time he heard that title. It was something earned, not just by her, but by the missing factor in his life. And now, he was accompanying her out in the middle of the ocean, fighting seasickness, doing everything except what he would rather be doing.

"Yes?"

"It's almost six. Time to embrace that sunrise."

He glared at his mother with glassy eyes. She was already dressed in her tan shorts, blue tank top, and a thin white jacket. Her hair was whipped up in a quick, ratty bun. She was not looking to impress anyone with her looks, and should she go diving later today, her hair would be messed up anyway, so there was no point in making it neat.

"And what exactly are we going to accomplish at this hour?" he moaned, hands rubbing over his eyes.

"A lot of things," she said with joy. "We're taking new water samples from the sea bottom. It's almost two miles deep down here. It's gonna take a while for the sub to get all the way down there, so we need to get started early."

She turned around and went topside, trusting Jon to drag himself out of his bunk and get decent.

Rising like the undead, he placed his feet on the deck and sat up. Groaning, he stood straight and lumbered to his closet. He opened the thin door carefully, worried he would break the cheap wood it was made from. The guys whom his mother chartered this boat from were real pieces of work. They were not too unpleasant to be around, but they were definitely on the lookout for more money. Two days ago, Jon had pulled the pantry door open with a little too much force, loosening the knob.

Not two seconds later, the boat's captain started going off on how that would be an extra hundred dollars to his fee.

Jon sorted through his belongings, choosing a pair of khaki shorts, a navy blue t-shirt, and fresh socks, and a red bandanna, previously worn by Brandon H. Otrin.

In that unpacked duffle bag where Jon had stuffed both his clean and dirty laundry, he saw a photo laying face-up. On it was an image of a man in an Army uniform standing next to a ten-year-old Jon, who wore kid-sized army fatigues, proudly emulating his dad.

It was an image that evoked several conflicting emotions. He enjoyed reminiscing of those days, but scowled when he remembered they were all in the past. Then came two shades of anger; the first from the cold, hard reality that his dad was no longer alive, and the second from Mom's insistence that Jon did not enlist. She had already lost her husband overseas, and was not keen on suffering that same anguish with Jon.

All of his life, he could not wait to turn eighteen, graduate high school, and sign up. From the age of six all the way to sixteen when his father was taken—at his nineteenth year of service, eighteen months from retirement—he spent time at shooting ranges and even joined a JROTC program, all with the goal of following in his dad's footsteps.

Mothers had a unique way of persuasion, and following her insistence, Jon could not bring himself to go into the service. That did not mean there was no resentment. As he'd found out in the few months following his eighteenth birthday, there was much of that to be had, and there was no sign of it going away. Instead of learning how to drop from a fast rope from a helicopter, he was instead going off the side of a boat in a tin can. It was an experience many would cherish, but Jon wanted none of it, for it was all at the cost of his true calling in life.

He covered the picture with his slept-in shirt and pants, then headed to the galley. After using the restroom and helping himself to some coffee and toast, he went topside.

It was still dark out. The sun was just starting to rise over the east. In fifteen minutes, a beautiful golden stream would encompass the *Kingsford* and the Andaman Sea. What most would consider a marvelous sight was only the start of another day in Jon's miserable existence.

He was not supposed to be here. It was not part of the goal. But here he was, coasting through life, trying to remind himself to embrace this time with his mother, but failing. He did not long for twenty years of service like his father did. He just wanted to join the Army and become part of a proud family tradition experienced by all the men in five generations of his family.

His mother's specialty was in marine biology. Since his dad's death, she grew more obsessive with the work. Jon knew it was her way of coping, especially since the G.I. bill enabled her to pursue her degree without significant debt. In these past two years, she threw herself in her work, not wanting to waste what Brandon Otrin had provided for her.

She stood on the main deck of the *Kingsford*, next to a small submersible called the *Trench Lightning*. It was a Triton sub, capable of plunging to depths of eight thousand feet, or slightly more than one-point-five miles.

Helping with the cable was the boat's captain and owner Ernie Cardellini. Though spending the last two decades in Thailand, he still had his East Maryland accent, where he was born and raised. From the ages of seventeen to forty, he worked on a sword boat, laying lines all across the Grand Banks the waters east. Tough financial times, and rumors of some criminal activity, somehow led him to the far east. Now, he worked and resided off the coast of Thailand, his free time spent in brothels and bars.

Those particular details were unknown to Tracie until she met with the guy. Had there been more grant money at her disposal, she would have tried to find a new charter. Unfortunately, time and money were not on her side. The submersible was only loaned to her because it was an old model. Though still functional and seaworthy, it was considered at the tail end of its lifespan.

Oliver, the first mate, sat at the observation deck, dangling a cigarette from his mouth while he watched the activity below.

“That’s an awfully expensive coffin,” he joked.

Tracie held still, on the verge of telling off the crusty, hundred-and-forty-pound fisherman. He had less class than Ernie, and was hell on the eyes. It was a rare occasion where the heavier guy was more appealing to look at than the skinny one. Ernie, while far from attractive, at least carried himself well. If one did not see him in his private time, he could easily be mistaken for someone with some measure of personal standard. Oliver did not even bother with that. His white shirt was dirty, his face badly in need of soap, and his hair crowning around the back of his otherwise bald head. His boots were well beyond their lifespan, as were his jeans. It was the same outfit he had worn yesterday and the day before, and he had the odor to show for it.

“Lucky for us, this one is a proven model,” she said. “It has gone far deeper than where we’re going.”

Oliver drew on his cigarette. “Yeah? For what? To me, it’s all an expensive joyride to see nothing but pitch black.”

Tracie was in the process of getting into the hatch when she answered. She did not know why she was engaging in this conversation. Maybe it was the fact she liked to teach and had a naïve hope she could educate the four-pack-a-day fisherman.

"There's more to that than darkness," she said. "It's a whole 'nother world down there. I've seen undersea mountain regions that rival the Rockys. There are deep trenches teeming with all kinds of life, many of which are yet to be discovered. Exploring the depths helps us understand the planet's geological history and allows us to discover new tectonic plates. These things matter because they can help us predict certain events, like undersea earthquakes, for example. Considering where you live, I think you can appreciate the importance of a new early warning system."

Oliver continued puffing smoke, his focus more on her legs than anything she had to say.

"Oh yeah," Jon muttered, barely loud enough to be heard. "We're totally making advances in the field of science. Hence the grant came from someone hoping to find new nickel deposits."

Tracie closed her eyes. It was the only way she could keep herself from giving her son a scowling look.

Indeed, their purpose in making these dives had little to do with marine research. In fact, should they find what their sponsor was looking for, it would have the opposite effect. As human beings existed, the need for materials persisted. Minerals used in everyday life did not just come from mines in Africa and Asia, but from under the water.

If there was any consolation in finding an underwater mineral deposit, it was knowing the company would not rely on foreign workers it could pay for slave wages to extract them. It would require skilled labor from people who would demand top dollar.

It was a small comfort, though. Tracie decided to focus on the fact it allowed her to conduct several dives into the little-known world at the seafloor.

She looked at her son. "You all set, Jon?"

"How long is this going to take?" he asked.

"As long as we need it to," she replied. "We're not out here on holiday. We're here to do a job. And I need your help operating the arms."

Jon exhaled, tempted to bum a cigarette from Oliver. He tried to focus on the kind words expressed by one of Tracie's colleagues, stating how he is one of the youngest, if not *the* youngest person to operate a DSV. Having a mother who was obsessed with this stuff had a hand in that.

Maybe he would appreciate it the older he got. For now, all he wanted was an M1 Carbine, fatigues, and an insignia on his arm.

But that was not to be.

He grabbed a water bottle and headed for the sub. Tracie went in ahead of him, cramming herself into the tight quarters. Jon went in behind her, scooching against her waist as he put himself in the co-pilot's seat.

"Be careful down there," Ernie called to them.

"Thanks, Captain," Tracie said. "We will."

"Hard to get paid if I bring you guys back smushed," he quipped. Not waiting for a reply, he sealed the hatch.

Tracie pursed her lips, wishing the company was not so cheap as to hire these guys. She would much prefer an actual research vessel equipped and designed for these kinds of expeditions. But now, she was stuck with these guys, on a boat that was clearly not hosed off after every fishing trip.

She took her son's hand. "Let's do this."

He gave her a half-hearted squeeze. "Yep."

Tracie sensed the displeasure in his voice. She looked over at him, mouth parted as though to say something. After a few seconds, she turned her eyes to the controls.

The crane lifted the *Trench Lightning* and brought it over the side. It was time to begin their work.

Jon watched the ocean splash against the porthole.

Mom's true pride and joy.

CHAPTER 3

"Target's on approach. Two vessels, just as we predicted. Speed is slowing. They appear to be taking the bait."

Kane Carpenter stayed low and quiet, keeping fifteen feet under the surface with his team. The six commandos were perfectly still and vertical, appearing like a small school of extremely dark jellyfish. In the daylight, they would stick out like a sore thumb. But they were still under the cover of darkness, watching the dark shape of the small fishing yacht swaying in the ocean current above them.

On board was Agent Ravee, the liaison assigned to their task by their client. Kane usually hated having to bring a third party on his missions. Usually, they slowed things down, tried to backseat drive the operation, and always posed a hazard. Should they get killed, the client would either cut the team's fee or do away with it entirely.

Ravee, to his credit, was one of the better ones. Unlike most agents, he actually respected Kane and proved to be a valuable resource. Having served with their target many years ago, he understood how the man operated.

Currently, he was aboard a small shrimp boat taken from his island nation of Malau.

That target was Daow Aree, a rising crime lord and pirate who was quickly gaining influence in the north Indian Ocean. His operation was still considered small, but his reach was quickly expanding, and the consequence of his business was starting to infect the coastal nations in Southeast Asia.

Heroin, specifically. What was joked about as being an American problem was quickly plaguing Thailand, Vietnam, China, and the Philippines.

Ironically, it was not any of these larger nations who decided to do something about it, but the small unknown island nation Malau, located near Thailand. When the son of a government official overdosed on the junk, Ravee, now a resident and government employee of this nation, was assigned to the case.

Ravee was savvy enough to know that, in order to eliminate the problem quickly, he would need to go straight for the source. To do that, they needed to skip the red tape and endless dialogues about borders and territories, and hire a private contractor who could operate without jurisdiction.

Approaching from the northeast were two yachts, their shapes dark compared to the brightening glow of the morning sunrise. They decreased in speed and approached Ravee's vessel.

"I've got a visual on three armed men on the vessel on the lefthand side. AK-47s. They're not afraid to brandish them. Just as we hoped, they think I'm some lowly fisherman who they can hijack. Pirates will be pirates."

Kane looked to the six men under his command. He pointed at Axel, Woodley, Berkley, and Vladik, then directed them to the boat on the lefthand side. Next, he nodded at Hatcher and Taft, pointing his thumb up to the second vessel. In their scuba gear, they all looked identical, but Kane knew each one of them like the back of his hand.

The group split into their two teams and ascended to the boats.

Kane brought himself to his boat's port aft side, his head emerging in the dawn's early light. He could hear the pirates shouting to one another and barking orders at Ravee, attempting to intimidate him into giving up his vessel and all of his belongings.

Hatcher and Taft emerged beside him.

Kane found the aft ladder and slowly pulled himself aboard, his suppressed HK MP7 submachine gun strapped over his right shoulder.

Peeking over the gunnel, he spotted one pirate on the aft deck. He was facing the opposite direction, trying to get a peek at what was going on in front of the boat. He held a machine pistol in one hand and had his other hand clenching his sheathed knife. Tattoos and scars decorated his body, illustrating a life of blood and violence. Like all of the other men aboard this boat, he was not some guy whose life had taken a bad turn. He was a career criminal. Worse, a plague, one who took joy in the harm he caused.

Much like Daow Aree.

As silent as a spider creeping on a wall, Kane moved over to the sentry. His left hand pulled a knife from his belt. The pirate was muttering something to himself, impatient with the back and forth taking place between the boat's captain and their new victim.

His yell was suppressed by a hand cupping over his mouth. Kane pulled him back, plunging his knife up at a forty-five-degree angle, through the back, into the heart.

The pirate groaned, then dropped his arms, dead.

Kane unslung his submachine gun and stood watch while Hatcher and Taft came aboard. They removed their masks, the former sporting his large white face, the latter a thinly trimmed beard.

They watched to the right, witnessing Vladik and Axel stealthily eliminate two sentries on the stern of their boat.

Kane looked at Hatcher and pointed to a ladder at the front of the deck. *Secure the bridge.*

Hatcher nodded and moved that way.

Kane and Taft formed up on the door and peeked through the window. There were three men in the passageway, all facing forward. Two of them were armed with assault rifles, the third empty-handed, with a pistol tucked in his pants.

After counting down from three, Kane opened the door.

Both mercs swarmed the interior of the vessel, Kane taking the two nearest to the right, Taft taking the one on the left. Suppressed shots delivered spiraling lead projectiles at terminal velocity, dropping all three targets before they could make a sound or return fire.

They checked the VIP guest cabin. Nobody there. Next was the aft bathroom. The man inside groaned at whoever was pestering him to wait his turn for the head.

Kane had no intention. He barged in and watched the pirate look up from his illicit magazine, his mouth dropping after seeing the muzzle pointed at him. A squeeze of the trigger dropped the booklet from his hands permanently, while simultaneously ending his tenure as a pirate.

They checked the navigation area. It was empty.

So far, there was no Daow.

If he was on this boat, he would be on the forward deck.

They heard someone calling out from that direction.

Kane and Taft checked their weapons.

"How's it going upstairs?" the commander asked Hatcher.

"All set. Ready to surprise the guys in the front. We better act fast. The captain is starting to notice his boat's a little quiet."

"Ah! That's what the commotion's all about. How many are up there?"

"Five. All heavily armed."

"Copy that. Stand by." Kane and Taft returned to the aft deck. On each side of them was a side deck running down the length of the yacht. "I'll take the port route, Taft take starboard. Set your timer for ten seconds. Hit the ones farthest out, we'll take the ones closest to the door. On my mark… mark."

"Mark."

"Mark."

The timer started.

Ravee, overhearing their dialogue, started blabbering something in Thai language, keeping their attention on him while the mercs got into position.

Kane and Taft split up and moved forward on opposite sides of the yacht.

By the time Kane neared the forward deck, his timer was at three.

He identified two pirates just a few feet away from him, standing side-by-side at thirty-degree angles, nearly facing one another. A little more to the starboard side was the guy who was doing the talking, and at the tip of the forward deck were two others, aiming weapons at the boat.

Zero.

Kane sprang into action, wrapping an arm around the neck of one of the pirates and using him as a human shield. The one next to him jumped back in shock, swinging his rifle barrel towards the intruder.

Kane fired, putting three large holes in the hostile's chest.

Taft emerged from his hiding spot and put a few rounds through the knees of the talkative one on the starboard gunnel, dropping him to the deck.

More shots, barely audible, spewed from Hatcher's weapon up on the flying bridge, popping holes in the last two pirates.

Kane, grasping his shield by the lower jaw, whipped his hand to the left.

SNAP!

The dead pirate faceplanted, his head crooked from its structural integrity having cracked like a toothpick.

Things were a tad messier on the other boat. A few assault rifle shots rang out while Vladik's team eliminated those on its bow deck. Woodley looked to his commander and lifted a thumbs up, confirming the boat to be secure.

Taft moved to the injured pirate, disarmed him, and lifted him by his hair for Ravee to get a look at him.

"This our guy?"

Ravee shook his head. "Nope. That's Jimmu, though. One of his top guys."

The pirate cursed at his captors, spitting at Kane's boots.

"Oh, you really showed him," Taft quipped.

Kane grabbed the prisoner by the jaw and made direct eye contact. "Speak English?"

Jimmu gave an animalistic smile. "A few words."

"Yeah? Such as?"

"Fuck you."

It was a response Kane anticipated. Right on cue, he placed his gun to the prisoner's forehead.

"Why don't you tell us where your boss is?"

"Who?" Jimmu said, playing dumb. "We're just out for a party."

"Some party," Taft said, bumping one of the dead men's assault rifles with his boot.

"We hear you like to cater certain parties," Kane said. "Hence the cargo you've been shipping out of this region. Heroin? Ring a bell?"

"What do you care?" the pirate snarled.

"It's not my job to care," Kane said. He tilted his head towards Ravee. "That's *his* job. Mine is to find your boss, Daow Aree. So, do yourself a favor and tell us where he is. If you do, then you can spend the next several years behind bars instead of being fish food."

Oddly enough, the prisoner looked more perplexed than anything else.

"You don't know where he is?"

Kane and Taft shared a glance.

"Kinda why we're asking you," Taft said. "Believe me, the boss isn't the kind of guy who wastes his time playing Twenty Questions if he doesn't have to. Especially if the other player is someone like you."

Jimmu was silent for a moment, a few strands of slobber dripping over the tattoo on his chin and neck. The guy seemed more surprised by the fact they did not already know his boss' location than he was at the surprise attack on his boat.

"You not know." It was more a statement of realization than a question.

Kane grabbed him by the hair. "Talk."

Jimmu shuddered in obvious fear. Something within Kane sensed that it was not a fear of his captors, but of betraying his own boss. In his mind, Daow was superior to these three men around him. Should he overcome the effort to bring him down, he would terminate anyone who assisted the enemy. Whether or not it was done willingly did not make a difference.

"You know what it's like to be skinned alive?"

Kane shook his head. "I keep mine pretty close."

Jimmu sniggered. "Won't be that way for long. For you or me. I saw him hang a naked man upside down once. He used a big knife and ran it down his body, slowly. There was a fire underneath him. It sizzled every time the blood dripped. Daow made it last for an hour, maybe longer, before he died. *That* is what will happen to you. But me?"

He threw himself to the side, grabbed ahold of one of his subordinate's rifles, and rolled on his back to aim it at the mercs. His last act of defiance ended predictably, with Kane and Taft carving him open with a spray of bullets.

"Damn it!" Ravee said.

Taft whistled. "Interesting. He seemed to think we should've already known where their base of operations is at."

"Almost as if he knew, or at least suspected, we were out here," Kane replied. "Or believed *somebody* was out here, causing trouble for Daow."

Agent Ravee brought his boat alongside theirs.

"What do you make of this?" Kane asked him. "Does any other agency have people on the hunt for your guy?"

Ravee shook his head. "Not at the moment. He's not considered a high-value target in their eyes. If someone else was out here, we'd know about it."

"What about rivals?" Taft asked. "I can't imagine this guy hasn't made enemies in low places."

"It's possible," Ravee replied.

"One thing's for sure." Hatcher reappeared on the flying bridge, looking down at them. In his hand was a small ceramic statue of Buddha. He let it drop to the deck, shattering at their feet. Among the pieces were small brown baggies. "These guys weren't on their way back from delivering their merchandise; they had only just left and were on their way back."

Kane did the math in his head. "Meaning they were ordered back by the boss."

"Maybe there is some other player involved," Taft said.

Through their earpieces came Vladik's East Ukrainian accent. *"Hate to interrupt, Commander, but we're picking up something on the radio. Someone deliberately asking for Jimmu. Sounds like they're in some sort of trouble."*

He put his microphone to the radio. Through the feed came a panicked voice, sounds of gunfire, and shattering glass.

"That doesn't sound like a potluck," Taft remarked.

Kane looked to Ravee. "It seems they've got another boat out there. Wanna come aboard and talk their lingo; pretend you're one of them? Get their coordinates and act like we're gonna come help?"

Ravee tossed him a line. "Help me aboard."

"Got it." Kane looked at the aft deck of the second yacht. "Berkley, take the agent's boat and head back to the atoll where we left the chopper. I want you on standby in case we need a little air support."

"Copy that."

Taft helped the agent secure his boat and pulled him onto the yacht. Ravee, still dressed in his raggy fisherman outfit, hurried into the yacht's radio room.

CHAPTER 4

When the sub hit the water, Jon Otrin saw nothing but black night with only the light of a thousand stars and the moon shining through the clear sky. Though he resented being all the way out here in the middle of the ocean, he could not deny the beauty of seeing the silver specks above him, beaming down through a sky void of air pollution.

The only reason the view was front and center in his mind now was the absolute darkness outside his porthole. It was all black. Deathly black. Enough so, it made him very uncomfortable. He did not think himself as someone who scared easily. Ever since the age of four, he preferred sleeping without a nightlight. It was not a goth thing; he did not consider himself edgy. Darkness was just the absence of light.

But even in the thickest darkness he had ever found himself in, there was always some light, whether it be the stars, a TV screen, a phone, or anything else. Only now did he truly have an idea what pitch black actually was.

Down here, the sun may as well have been on the opposite side of the galaxy. There was no photosynthesis down here, no vegetation, no night or day. The only constant was the black and the crushing pressure. The latter was an element which separated this alien world from the rest of the planet. Only sperm whales ventured this deep, and only for a brief amount of time for hunting. Submarines had to be specially designed for such trips, or else face cataclysmic implosions. It was for that very reason Tracie quadruple checked every inch of the sub and ran multiple diagnostics prior to deployment. She may have been eager to conduct her deep dives, but she was not an idiot. After all, the best part of experiencing Mother Nature's darkest regions was coming back to tell about it.

"You are awake, right Jon?" she said.

"Yes, Ma."

"Just making sure. You've hardly said a word since we started." Her lips pressed together. "Actually, you've hardly said a word since we've been out here in general."

Jon watched the porthole. With hardly any lights inside the cockpit, he didn't even have his own reflection to look back on. Just the void, resembling outer space, only without the stars.

"Haven't really had much to talk about."

Tracie nodded. "You're mad at me. I'm not dumb, Jon. I know what's on your mind." Getting no reply from him, she turned her eyes to her instrument panel. "We're at seven-nine-four-nine. Go ahead and switch on forward and aft."

"Switch on what?"

"The lights," she replied.

"Oh." Jon searched through the various switches, forcing himself to recall his training that he so unenthusiastically took in preparation for this trip.

Strong white streams extended from two points on the sub's bow and one from its stern. By now, the *Trench Lightning* resembled an alien craft hovering above a barren mountain range.

Little specks darted in and out of the starboard beam, disappearing as quickly as they appeared.

"The hell are those?"

"Shrimp," his mother replied.

"Oh." He aimed that light down, finding a large, bumpy seabed underneath them. The rock, too, appeared pitch black, almost making it impossible to get a view of its topography. In reality, he was looking at a vast series of rolling hills and even some cliffs.

It was a huge canyon, one that was believed to store all kinds of minerals.

"I wanna get a sample," Tracie said. "Start the drill, will ya?"

"You sure it'll be alright?" he asked.

She lowered the sub to the top of one of those hills below them. "Yep. It'll be perfectly fine."

He grabbed the joystick, watching the glow outside his porthole. Funnily enough, having an actual visual of the place was worse than not being able to see anything at all. Something about the way the light penetrated the abyss made him think of some horrendous aftermath, such as nuclear winter, and this little machine was his safehouse. Outside that window was death, but instead of radiation, it was pure brute force from above. Simple weight, more powerful than any environment imaginable, save for those of deeper water.

The condensation within the cockpit was not helping matters. His own sweat began to wet his father's bandanna, making him pull it off to avoid soiling it. His hair popped out from under the fabric, in a wild, shaggy state from being pressed against his pillow all night.

"Oh, lord," Tracie joked. "You really do need a haircut."

She hoped to get a laugh from her son, only to be disappointed by the usual blank expression. He worked the starboard arm and applied the drill to the sediment.

A faint *ZERRRR* noise could be heard through the hull while the bit dug several inches deep.

"Good, good," Tracie said. "Let's collect the sample, and we'll move on."

"How will we know if this contains any metals?" he asked.

Tracie perked up, suddenly feeling delighted. He actually spoke on his own volition for once. Not only that, but there seemed to be minor interest in what they were doing.

"What you're drilling into isn't just some hill," she said. "It's a nodule. We discovered them when conducting our undersea mapping. Often, they contain nickel and cobalt. What we're actually getting a sample of is the crust, which we'll bring topside and find out if there are any of these elements located within it."

She was a little disappointed when she heard her son's usual "Oh" response.

Jon successfully collected the rock sample that was actually crust.

Tracie elevated the sub two meters and pushed forward.

"How many more are we going to take?" he asked.

Tracie's brief enlightened feeling was gone. She had hoped she could bond with her now-adult son out here. Maybe even get him enthusiastic about pursuing a career in marine biology or underwater geology. In her fantasy, they could keep going on expeditions, traveling the world together, seeing all sorts of different things, and even make a few discoveries.

They were not off to a good start.

"There's at least eight more locations I wanted to look at. Three of them are nearby."

"Mm."

Tracie exhaled slowly. While she understood her son's mindset and sympathized with it to an extent, those 'response sounds' as she called them, were getting tiresome.

She kept to the task, bringing their submersible fifteen degrees port to check out their next spot.

Jon, as usual, watched the light through the porthole. "What are those?"

She looked, then lit up with excitement. In the glow of their light were a pair of creatures that resembled large moths.

"Yeti crabs!"

"Ah." He nodded. "Thought they were bugs."

She chuckled. "Yeah, they look like bugs, don't they?"

Jon aimed his light farther out. "There's a few of them."

"Maybe they found a place to feed," she said.

Jon panned the light far out. "Is that a nodule?"

"Hmm?"

"Out there. Looks like they're gathering near one of those nodules you were talking about," he said.

Tracie throttled back and turned to starboard, bringing the object into the glow of the port spotlight.

For a minute, she sat perfectly silent and still.

"That's not a nodule."

They both looked at the object's rounded bottom and the pointed tip at its front. Scattered across the seafloor around it were hundreds of different objects, with different textures, shapes, sizes, and mass.

On its end was a spiral object, comprised of metal. A propeller.

"That's a boat," she said.

Jon felt his sweating intensify. "We're looking at a shipwreck?"

Tracie brought the sub closer, observing all of the fragments around it. Its hull was compressed and lined with all sorts of deep, narrow markings. In its center was a gap, the metal around it caved inward.

It was not damage consistent with an implosion. It was too narrow. Too *precise*, looking more like a giant pair of wire cutters had clamped down on the hull. The rest appeared as though someone had lashed the boat with huge strands of barbed wire.

"The crabs are certainly interested," Jon said.

"Probably feeding on the bodies and any rations in the galley," Tracie replied.

Jon gulped and sank in his seat.

Tracie cringed, hoping she didn't put his stomach past the point of no return. They had barf bags, but while they prevented a bad mess, they failed to contain the smell. In a tight space like this, such an odor would accumulate like a thick fog.

"Sorry. Drink some of your water."

Jon waved his hand. "I'm good." He exhaled sharply, regaining control, and sat up. Watching the wreck outside, he took notice of a few of the crustaceans near a breach in the stern. They were upside down, motionless…dead. “Hmm. I think some of them ate too much.”

Tracie saw what he was looking at, her face twisting with confusion.

“Odd.”

“What? Crabs don’t die?” Jon said. “I’ve attended plenty of seafood dinners that beg to differ.”

“Very funny.” The more she looked, the more dead crabs she discovered. They were not torn apart as though attacked by a predator, but completely intact. One or two dead ones, especially in a group, was nothing concerning, but in this gathering, there were at least twelve dead, and a few other ones acting a little lethargically.

“I want to check this out,” she said.

“What? The crabs?” Jon asked. “You think something on the boat is killing them?”

Tracie nodded. “We need water samples and a couple of the bodies.”

“What do you think it is?” Jon asked. “Fuel?”

She shook her head. “Chemicals. Either it’s something that’s in the water, or something they consumed. Either way, I want to know.”

There was a hint of relief on Jon’s face. As it turned out, they would be heading topside sooner than expected.

CHAPTER 5

The beach was silent, everyone around it watching the pirate leader gaze upon the ravaged shack. Many of the docks on this side of the island had been ripped away, their legs uprooted, the personnel on watch gone, with only the exception of a few severed limbs that now served as breakfast for birds and crabs inhabiting the shores.

Daow Aree watched the aftermath with red eyes—literally, in the case of the left one. A blood clot from three years back had left it permanently bloodshot. It was a condition that usually left a person's eyes pasty white from blindness. While the blindness was true, he had the rare exception in color. Some say he was special. Others speculated his shoulder had been touched by the devil.

Daow preferred that second explanation. Given the severity of what had occurred overnight, he was itching to lend his abyssal friend a hand and deliver some souls straight to hell.

First on that list was looking to be Rudy Li, a man he believed to be his ally. Now, the drug lord had serious questions regarding his loyalty and competence.

The owner of the small petroleum company stationed on this island had made sure to take a piss before accompanying Daow and his men to the south shore. He was glad too, as he would otherwise have humiliated himself in the presence of the pirates.

After what felt like a decade of silence, Daow finally spoke.

"Explain this to me."

Rudy quivered. "I don't know."

Daow looked at him, deliberately keeping his dead, red eye in the petroleum executive's peripheral vision. Rudy could not bring himself to look right at him, feeling as though that eye would possess his soul.

"What do you mean you don't know? You ensured me nobody comes through here except your people and mine. That nobody had reason to investigate your island."

"And that's the truth," Rudy said. "Unless somebody from your group screwed up, you know, by hijacking a ship and getting themselves traced back here, nobody knows of our operation."

He bit his lip, thinking he may have been a little too brave with that statement.

Adding to his nervousness was the way Daow's right-hand man, Goro, strutted behind him. The man was a brute, both in physicality and temperament. Some say he was able to kill a man by crushing his skull in with his bare hands. Just looking at his face was enough to convince Rudy the guy was capable of such things. Worse than capable, he was *willing*.

"If I may…"

Another man stepped up. It was Eiji, often referred to as Daow's trusted advisor. For a band of ruthless pirates and drug dealers, he didn't quite match the stereotypical appearance. He was somewhat well-dressed, usually sporting clean pants or shorts, and often wore a white or blue shirt with a buttoned collar. Today, it was blue.

"Yes?" Daow said. He always sounded impatient with Eiji, but always gave him the time of day.

"I do agree that this is peculiar," the advising pirate said. "But, if it was a strike force, would they not have pressed the attack inland after taking down our outposts?"

Daow nodded, having considered this factor for himself.

"I'll admit, they would've had the drop on us. At the same time, I highly doubt the hand of God came down and ravaged our guards."

"Fair enough," Eiji said. "Perhaps it was someone else; someone with limited manpower, but who still wanted to mess with us. Maybe even draw us out in hopes of setting us up for a surprise attack?"

Daow thought about it for a minute.

"Chao Fah. He's been trying to cut into my territory for the last year. Twice I've had to send a message with the bodies of his dealers. We know for a fact he tried moving his product through this area. That boat we sunk with his people on it." He looked at Rudy. "Possibly looking for the cover and luxury of having a petroleum refinery to do his work in."

"I've talked to nobody," Rudy pleaded. "I swear, I know nothing about this."

"What about that boat with the submarine on its deck?" Goro suggested. "They've been hanging around a while. It's possible they've seen some of our activity."

"That doesn't add up," Eiji said. "No way would any agency send a group like that, knowing our reputation. That'd be like sending a sheep to spy on the wolves."

"Unless they know we're trying to keep a low profile," Daow said. He rolled his jaw, munching on some seeds while he pondered. "It's the only thing that makes even a lick of sense. Like you said, maybe they're trying to bait us, first with a boat with a lot of supplies… and a pretty woman… but also these obvious attacks on our watch posts."

The other pirates nodded. Even Goro would dare not outright disagree with the leader.

"What will you do?" Rudy asked, beads of sweat rolling over his nose.

Daow looked at the horizon. Near that infinite line in the distance where the sea connected with the sky was a grey speck. A boat, where the supposed scientist was aboard.

"Mount up. Let's pay them a little visit."

Like an army prepping to go to war, the pirates on the shoreline moved inland. They collected weapons and ammo, then went to the east dock where their strikers were moored.

Rudy stood, nervous about the ramifications. He was more than happy to get involved in Daow's drug trade as long he got paid his cut. Being the executive of a small, but profitable company that provided the band of pirates housing and cover, he was in a unique position where Daow could not afford to simply terminate him. However, the reality of such an alliance was weighing on him. Real people, probably innocent people, were about to get hurt. And he could do nothing about it. He may have been useful, but he was not immune. If Daow considered him to be compromised or more trouble than he was worth, he would get the bullet, and the pirates would simply find a new location to do their work.

He could do nothing but stand and watch while Daow and his band of cutthroats mounted up and set out to do what they did best: pillage.

CHAPTER 6

"Well… did not expect this."

Axel's voice traveled far and wide, not requiring the use of comms to get his message across.

The two yachts drifted five meters apart from one another, the seven men gazing in awe of the wreckage in front of them. The vessel that carried another crew of Daow Aree's pirates was half-submerged and leaning to starboard. Its mast was broken in the middle, the hull crumbled in various locations, and its bridge torn apart.

Its main deck had been ripped open, its guts torn out like paper pulled from inside of a gift bag.

Agent Ravee, now dressed in similar tactical clothing as his contractors, stood on the flying bridge of the yacht, whose name translated to *Grand Voyager,* observing the strange aftermath of whatever had occurred here.

"You sure you didn't hear any information on the radio?" Kane asked him.

Ravee nodded. "The radioman gave me the coordinates, said they were being attacked, and before he could say more, the radio went dead."

Taft whistled. "Shit. Somebody did a number on this. Whoever it is, they've got a serious bone to pick with Daow. I mean, look! They blew its deck wide open."

Hatcher shook his head. "You're suggesting they used a bomb. First of all, there are no powder marks. Second of all, look at the way the hull is bent inward and how the structure is caving *outward.* It's been crushed *and* ripped apart."

Taft sniggered at that. "Okay, fine. I did notice that, and I do find it odd, but you're not gonna convince me somebody rolled up to this thing, attached a few crane cables to it, and ripped its deck open."

"Then disappeared without a trace," Kane added. He exhaled sharply. He hated mysteries and anomalies. Often, they suggested a new player in the game. Given the number of enemies Daow had made in his life, it stood to reason someone else was out here hunting him down. For someone to do a number on his shipping vessels like this, it would've had to be someone who hated his guts.

The second yacht, the *Saint Nicholas*, was a few yards closer to the wreckage, the two mercs aboard waiting for Vladik.

He popped up after exploring the interior.

"Any bodies?" Kane called to him.

"No," Vladik replied after removing his rebreather. He raised a statue. "I did find plenty of these. A couple were broken."

Taft sniggered. "Surprised we can't see a bunch of little baggies floating around." He shrugged. "Maybe they sank."

"Yeah, maybe," Kane said. He turned to his left, watching the vast ocean all around them. He had hoped the hardest part of this assignment would be locating the pirate camp. That alone was bound to be a challenge. There were several small islands in this region, and they did not have the resources to properly search them all. Doing flybys with the chopper would not do much good either, for Daow could easily spot it from afar, enabling him to plan a surprise attack or relocate.

Now, it was clear there was someone else killing the pirates. Whoever it was, they weren't after the heroin. That, or they somehow didn't know the product was located inside those little statues. Unlikely, but then again, anything was possible.

"It's a good thing we packed the special hardware."

Everyone on his team knew what he was referring to. In addition to their rifles, submachine guns, grenades, and diving equipment, they had packed a special tool supplied to them from an old, retired buddy of Kane's. Nicknamed 'Shooting Star', he was an old man in a profession where many died young. He would have gladly kept going, but had the good sense to know his body could not keep up with the career any longer, and would only be a hazard to his men. Not only was Shooting Star a hell of a warfighter, but he had connections. Among them were weapons manufacturers, who provided him models of some of the newest stuff being produced.

Because he was 'such a nice guy', he gifted Kane Carpenter with his favorite toy, affectionately referred by him as the 'Supernova'. It was a dumb, cheesy title given by the man himself, stating that it would come at the target like a shooting star, then go supernova on contact.

In essence, it was a homing missile launcher and targeting system.

There was plenty to mock ol' Shooting Star for, but if anyone had earned such antics, it was him. Kane knew better than to poke fun at him. The guy had hired Kane when he got out of the Marine Corps and entered the private sector. Under him, Kane learned far more than he ever did in the service.

During their takeover of the yachts, it was stowed away in the fishing boat Ravee distracted the pirates with. Now, it was on the *Grand Voyager*, having been brought along as a precaution. It brought to mind the phrase 'better to have one and not need it than need it and not have one.'

"We're still in a bit of a pickle, Commander," Hatcher said. "We still have no idea where our objective is."

"I wouldn't say we have no idea," Taft chimed in. "He's gotta be in this area somewhere. All three of these boats were intending to gather in the same area. The ones we're standing on now were heading southwest, and this wrecked one was heading south. All we need is a map and a pencil, and we can get an estimate of where they were going."

It was a simple, yet good observation.

Agent Ravee brought a map out of the pack and unfolded it over the console.

"We're here," he said, pointing a finger to a blue spot of ocean. He ran his finger a few inches to the east. "We took these yachts this way, and they were heading at a heading of zero-eight-five. Unfortunately, we can't know the precise heading of the hunk of junk in front of us, but if I were to venture a guess…." He took a pen and drew a couple of lines. "I'd say they were heading this way."

The two lines converged near a small cluster of islands thirty degrees southwest of their present location.

"Quite a few islands there," Hatcher said.

"It still narrows it down," Kane said.

Taft pointed to a speck of land marked as *Coral Basin* on the map. "What about this one? That looks like a decent spot to set up camp."

"It's possible," Ravee said.

Kane, on the other hand, was not so convinced.

"What's with this island here?" he asked, pointing to an island a couple miles west of Coral Basin, called Rook Island. "Looks like it's marked as an industrial site."

"It is," Agent Ravee said. "There's a man from my country who operates a petroleum manufacturing plant there. They run a few oil rigs in the area."

"Have they reported any suspicious activity?"

Ravee thought about it for a moment. "No."

The way he spoke indicated a lightbulb had gone off in his head. At first, it seemed unlikely that a major company—major for the small island nation—would risk everything to get on board with the drug business. But the more he thought about it, the more it made sense. Ravee's country valued the petroleum plant, for it brought much needed income and supplied jobs to many of its citizens. The government would be very reluctant to even accuse the CEO or any of the company executives of illicit activities without substantial evidence.

But money meant power, and the guys running the company loved both. Sadly, there was much money in the world of narcotics, and greater wealth would allow the company to expand.

Ravee crumpled the map, hating himself for not making the connection earlier. "I was so focused on that pirate bastard that I didn't consider outside factors. But you're right, we should head there first."

"Speaking of outside factors," Taft said, "I'm still a tad worried about *this.*" He was looking at the yacht wreckage. "Let's not forget, there's someone else out here presumably with a grudge against Daow. Given how sloppy this new player is, I would not be surprised if that guy is aware that someone's out to spoil his day. Meaning, he's probably a little more on edge than usual."

"Making a sneak attack a little tougher to conduct," Hatcher added.

Kane tapped the console. "Using their own boats will help us with that. Agent Ravee can do the talking, since he knows how these guys operate."

Taft chuckled. "Plus, he looks and sounds like 'em."

The agent glared at him.

Kane, grimacing, shook his head. "If you want to deck him, you've got my full permission. Just don't hurt him too bad until after we finish the job."

Taft looked at his boss as though he had summoned him to be put up for ritual sacrifice.

"Holy crap, Commander."

Hatcher snorted. "You asked for it, dumbass."

Ravee lightened up. “Technically, he’s right. I just hope I can keep them fooled long enough for us to dock and get a foothold on the place.”

“First thing’s first…” Kane looked to the other boat. “Woodley?”

The merc with the beanie turned to make eye contact. “Yes, Commander?”

“Get your drone in the air. Use your map. Primary location for recon is a place called Rook Island. Get an eye on the place and its surrounding waters. Link the feed to my tablet. In the meantime, that’s the course we’ll be setting for our boats.”

“Aye-aye,” those aboard the *Saint Nicholas* replied.

Kane got on his comm. “Berkley, you better not be taking any naps over there.”

“Who? Me?”

“Very funny. We have a possible location on the target. Be ready to join the fun.”

“Copy that.”

Woodley got right to work connecting the drone’s feed to the tablets. It was light blue in color with shades of white, enabling it to blend in with the clear sky. With a range of twelve miles, it helped drastically during searches, though its battery life left a little to be desired.

The machine took off into the air like a toy plane, quickly disappearing against the blue sky.

Both yachts pointed southwest and followed the drone, their occupants readying themselves for a firefight.

CHAPTER 7

"You know, there's better ways to deshell a crab, lady." Oliver, sporting his seventh cigarette for the day, pulled up a stool and sat over Tracie's left shoulder while she did analysis on the dead marine specimens pulled from the water. She and Jon had managed to collect three of the dead crabs found near the wreckage. Before ascending, Tracie decided to venture north closer to the drop off.

It was there they found the body of a dead shark, recently deceased, with no signs of physical damage aside from the small critters that were beginning to help themselves to it. Finding a dead animal in the water was, in itself, as common as finding an ant in a front lawn. But Tracie had a gut feeling it was related to the shipwreck and whatever was killing those crabs and shrimp.

It was tricky, but she was able to connect a cable to the specimen and have the boat hoist it up.

"Jon? Get me the ten millimeter syringe," she said to her son. Jon stood up from the cooler he sat on and went below to the makeshift lab his mother had set up in her cabin.

On the deck in front of her was one of the crabs, its shell carefully opened up in the middle, exposing its gooey innards.

"You're performing an autopsy?" Captain Ernie Cardellini asked. He joined his first mate for a smoke and watched the scientist prod at the crustacean's insides with some surgical utensils.

"Of sorts," she replied. "Technically, it's a necropsy."

"What's the difference?" Oliver asked.

"In short, autopsy is for humans, and necropsy is used for animals," she explained, her eyes fixed on the specimen the entire time.

Oliver took a long draw of his smoke. "So, it's an autopsy." He sniggered. "What is it with language and coming up with different words to describe essentially the same thing?"

Ernie, despite chuckling at his first mate's remarks, appeared to take a greater interest in what the scientist was looking at.

"It looks normal to me," he said. "What are you looking for, exactly?"

Tracie leaned away. "This."

She pointed at the crab's exposed stomach. Ernie leaned forward for a closer look, then shrugged. To him, the only time he had seen the inside of any crab was after it had been boiled or steamed.

Recognizing this fact, she opted to explain in layman's terms. "There's tissue damage inside of its stomach. There's scar tissue on its lining, as well as in the heart. Meaning this crab, the others we found down there, and the shark, consumed something hazardous from the ship. Whatever it was, it was ingestible and their bodies could not handle it."

Oliver looked at the shark. Its body was untouched by the doctor. No autopsy… or necropsy… had been performed.

"How do you know the shark suffered the same fate?"

Tracie exhaled. If she were to give the benefit of the doubt, maybe the guy was too busy to notice her performing a scan with a vascular ultrasound. It was hard to believe, given the way he was constantly eyeballing her.

"I was able to get images of its circulatory system," she explained. "The shark has collapsed veins and what appears to be an infection in its heart. Plus, there are abscesses on its liver. We don't often see this sort of thing in marine animals."

"So, what now?" Ernie asked. "Still gonna cut the shark open?"

Tracie nodded. "I might be able to get a look at the contents of its stomach and get a clue as to what they ate. But first, I want to get blood samples. Speaking of which… Jon! Where's that syringe?"

Running feet echoed below deck. A moment later, Jon arrived topside and approached his mother. In his hand was a large plastic cannister with an equally large needle.

"I couldn't find it. The only one I could locate was this one."

Tracie groaned. "How could you not find the others? They were kept in the same place."

"Hey, fire me," he shot back.

Tracie held her breath, and her words. Forcing herself to cool down, she extended her hand.

"It's alright. That'll work. Thank you."

She took the syringe and dug its needle into the shark's neck. Slowly, she extracted a few millimeters of blood.

Now, it was off to the microscope. She moved to the side of the deck where she had erected a small canopy to keep out the excess sunlight from her small white machine.

She put some of the blood on a plastic sheet and placed it under the lens.

Everyone on the ship waited quietly while she did her science stuff. After a couple of minutes, she looked up.

"No microorganisms." She stood up with her sample of blood and went below to her lab, leaving the three men topside.

Jon spent his time watching the horizon, pondering, fantasizing; his mind anywhere but here.

"All you're lacking are some twin suns," Oliver joked.

Ernie gave a scolding look to his first mate. "Hey you; remember how you promised to repair the ice machine?"

Oliver lowered his cigarette. "Aww."

"That's right. Get to it."

Seeming more like a rebellious, grumpy teenager even more than the literal one on their ship, Oliver strutted off, dragging his feet.

Jon kept watching the water, his eyes glazed over, their lids slumping from a lack of energy.

"Can't say the idiot is wrong, though," Ernie said out of the blue.

Jon looked at him. "Excuse me?"

"About you looking off into the horizon." Ernie took a minute to get his voice low and frog-like. "Never his mind on where he was. Hm? What he was doing."

Jon cracked a smile. Like many people, he appreciated a good *Star Wars* reference.

"My point… not that it's my place," Ernie continued, "is not to brush off your mom. Take it from me, kid. She's the only one you've got. And you never know for how long."

Jon was tempted to reply how well he understood that fact. After all, it was precisely what he experienced with his father. Life was normal and good. Sure, his dad was gone frequently for deployments, but they kept in touch regularly, and there was the knowledge that retirement was on approach. Additionally, Jon liked visiting the military bases and meeting the other soldiers. It was in his blood, and the idea of joining those warriors was something he yearned for.

It was 'Mommy' who kept him away from that.

"I lost my dad to a fishing accident when I was fifteen," Ernie continued. That got Jon's attention.

"Yeah?"

"Mmhmm." The captain took a draw of his smoke while he reflected on his younger days. "I thought that was bad enough at the time. You'd think I would've learned my lesson; that life can take something away from you in the blink of an eye. But I didn't. I was eighteen when my mother suffered a stroke. She didn't keep the best diet. The stress of being alone all the time didn't help. I was out working, wasn't bothering with school, and chasing after the ladies. During all of that, I wasn't paying attention to the one who was actually important. By the time I realized that, it was too late."

Jon sat in silence, slowly taking in what the captain was trying to say. Initially, his teenaged instinct to be rebellious and argue against those points welled up. Thanks to the art of self-control, he managed to shut that part of his mindset down in favor of a particular skill his dad had instilled in him.

"No matter how sure you are that you're right, always assume there's a possibility you may be wrong."

He looked at Ernie and gave a slight grin. It was a gesture that spoke a thousand words, all in appreciation.

True to his old sense of humor, he couldn't just say 'thank you'. It had to have a special touch to it.

"You know, for a guy who we found in a whorehouse, you actually have a few decent insights."

Ernie spat out his cigarette in laughter. "I have my moments."

For the next minute or two, they relished in the moment of levity, the young man taking on an unexpected appreciation of the overweight fisherman with poor hygiene.

Their smiles slowly shrank as both of them noticed a few imperfections in the perfect view of the north.

Ernie moved to the edge of the boat. "What do we have here?"

Jon put a hand over his eyes to block the sun. "Are those boats?"

"Yeah," Ernie said.

Jon noticed the apprehension in the captain's voice.

"That's normal, right? I mean, we're on the water. Boats tend to travel through the water."

"Yeah, but two strikers and a couple of skiffs? All in a group?"

"Boats don't travel in groups?" Jon asked.

"If they were heading straight west or east, I wouldn't think much of it," Ernie replied. "But they're coming straight at *us*."

Jon suddenly felt antsy. "What does that mean?"

Ernie did not answer straight away. He climbed up to the wheelhouse, reemerging a few seconds later on the observation deck with a pair of binoculars. He peered through the glasses. When he lowered them, he was alive with angst.

"Oliver!" he shouted through a two-way radio. "Get up here. We've got trouble."

"What is it?" Jon said. "What's happening?"

As he spoke, Tracie arrived on deck, simultaneously troubled yet enlightened, having made a discovery after testing the shark's blood.

"That's an interesting turn of events," she said. "Looks like our shark is a junkie, as are these crabs. That boat we found? Looks like they were in the business of shipping heroin."

She noticed the visible state of alarm her son and the boat captain were in.

"We've got another turn of events, Doctor," Ernie called down. He went into the wheelhouse and started up the boat's engine.

With a pointed finger, Jon directed his mother's attention to the group of boats coming their way.

Tracie sucked in a breath. "Oh, shit."

"You said there were drugs in the shark's system?" Jon asked.

"Yeah," she replied. "A lot, too. It overdosed, as did the crabs."

Jon connected the dots in his brain. "And we wandered into the middle of some guy's territory." He watched the boats close the distance. As they came within a few hundred feet, their assault rifles could be plainly seen.

Oliver arrived on deck and took a look at their visitors. "No, no, no! Not good." He started climbing up to the structure. "Pirates!"

"Are there usually pirates out this way?" Jon called to him. "Would've been nice to know beforehand."

"No," Oliver responded. "These guys are new."

Jon cocked his head back with a dumbfounded, "Oh!"

Gunshots cracked the air, making the first mate slide down the ladder. He hit the deck and ducked for cover.

Bullets struck the ship, the pirates not bothering with precise aim.

Jon, remembering his father's training to go for cover, grabbed his mother and forced her to the deck. They lay flat, hands over their heads, inches from the vile-smelling dead crabs.

After a very long thirty seconds, the shooting stopped. The boats circled the *Kingsford* like sharks circling a wounded whale.

One of the pirates yelled in a deep, husky voice. He called to the boat in Thai, and when he got no response, he switched to English.

"Show yourselves! Do it now, or we start shooting!"

Ernie appeared on the observation deck, hands raised.

"We didn't see you. Don't know you exist. Please, just let us go."

The pirates started laughing.

"Tell your crew to stand up," the lead pirate called out.

Ernie motioned to his first mate and his passengers. Reluctantly, they pushed themselves to their feet.

Rocking beside the *Kingsford* was one of the twenty-foot boats. On its deck, a large man stood with a rifle in hand.

"Stay where you are. We are going to board."

Lines with hooks were tossed over the gunnel, securing a hold. Like crusaders scaling the walls of a castle, they boarded the *Kingsford*.

Immediately, Tracie and Jon found themselves at gunpoint. Keeping their hands raised, they kept perfectly silent and prayed for some sort of divine intervention.

Jon felt sick, watching the way some of those scrawny pirates were looking at his mother. It was obvious what was on their minds, and it tempted him to snatch one of those assault rifles and lay waste to the entire clan.

The tall, muscular pirate set foot on the ship. Unlike the others, he appeared more reserved and focused, not letting himself get distracted by the thoughts of abhorrent activities involving their sole female prisoner.

He barked orders to some of the other pirates, who immediately began sweeping the interior of the vessel.

"What are you doing here?" he said to Tracie. "What is your purpose?"

Her lip quivered, reeling from the sudden turn in events. Never in her life had she experienced looking at the business end of a gun, let alone be taken hostage by a gang of very violent people who clearly lacked morality.

"Talk!" the pirate shouted.

"We're conducting research," Jon said on his mom's behalf. "We're marine biologists. We've been assigned to take sediment samples from the ocean floor, specifically the deep region past the drop-off." He hoped that was enough to satisfy the invader, but judging by the way he scowled at them, it was not.

One of the pirates pushed Ernie to the ladder as a way of saying, "Get your ass down there."

He joined his three companions near the submersible, keeping his hands where they could be seen.

A minute later, one of the pirates arrived after sweeping through the boat's interior.

"Goro, nobody else inside," he said in English.

The large man named Goro nodded at the wheelhouse. "Bring the boat to the east dock and take the others around the far side of the island. Dock them at the northwest pier."

His subordinate climbed to the wheelhouse and seized control of its helm.

Goro looked over the side at the two skiffs. "Ban-Jen, stay out here for a little longer. Use your radio and alert us if you find anything new."

The pirate, Ban-Jen, replied in Thai.

Goro turned around and kept his rifle pointed at the hostages. "We'll find out what you're really up to."

Jon's brow furrowed. "What? What do you mean?"

"Shh!" Ernie hissed.

Taking the captain's advice, the young man kept his mouth shut. For now, all he could do was wait while the pirates steered the *Kingsford* to the north, escorted by the two strikers, leaving the men on the skiffs to continue searching the nearby area.

He looked to the heavens, hoping to see some sort of sign that the Lord above had a plan to get them out of this mess. Jon was not one to pray often. He wasn't really sure what his spiritual beliefs were. But as his father had once pointed out, when he was in a pinch, he suddenly found himself talking to the man upstairs.

"Sometimes, it worked. Or, at least it seemed to work," he had said.

All Jon saw was clear blue sky, with a faint speck moving across it.

Probably a bird.

Not exactly the sign I was looking for.

***

"Whoa!" Woodley exclaimed through the radio channel. *"Score one for my eagle. We've got a positive ID on some pirate fiends."*

Kane and Ravee watched the aerial footage on the screen of his portable monitor. The drone's camera was able to zoom down heavily onto the deck of the vessel being hijacked.

"That's Goro," Ravee said, pointing to the muscular pirate leading the group. "He's Daow's right-hand man. His muscle, as you Americans like to put it."

"Quite literally, in this guy's case," Taft remarked, catching a peek at the scumbag.

"They're heading north," Kane said.

"Rook Island is right in their path," Ravee said.

"We were right." Kane watched the four prisoners aboard the eighty-foot fishing vessel, taking notice of the small submarine taking up much of the space on the deck. "And timely. These friendlies found themselves in Daow's crosshairs."

"We better act fast," Ravee said.

Kane took over the controls and put the *Grand Voyager* in full-throttle, the mercs aboard the *Saint Nicholas* doing the same.

"They have hostages," the commander said. "We're gonna need to be extra careful this time. They'll have the prisoners on land before we get there. Our best bet is to dock near the friendly vessel and eliminate all sentries around it. Woodley, try and get a reading on the island so we can come up with a proper battle-plan. One way or another, we're getting those hostages out of there."

Agent Ravee nodded in agreement.

"You are correct. I know how Daow's mind works. Those people are as good as dead. Either they die in the firefight, or Daow kills them later. Later would be worse, especially for the lady."

"Fortunately for them, they won't have to die at all," Kane said. He glanced at Hatcher. "Be ready with your sniper rifle. When the shit hits the fan, you'll have maybe a five-second window to take out any pirates near the hostages."

Hatcher smiled while picking his teeth with his knife. "Usually it's three."

CHAPTER 8

Ban-Jen took his skiff west, bring his crew out of the deep waters of the drop-off toward the shallower area near the island of Coral Basin, east of Rook Island. He, as well as his fellow pirates, were disappointed of the fact they would not get to witness Daow do what he did best.

There was a sick enjoyment in watching their leader hang somebody by their feet and dangle their head six inches over a bonfire. Even the toughest of individuals would thrash and cry like children, begging for an end to the torture. Daow would not end their misery there. Oh, no. That was when the fun was only just beginning.

And that was with common everyday hostages. The ones Goro was taking back to Rook Island potentially held information as to what occurred on the south shoreline last night. "I don't know" was not going to suffice as an answer.

His fellow pirates, Kiet and Anada, watched their surroundings, looking for signs of a helicopter or other vessels nearby. They were still high off the thrill of taking over the *Kingsford.* It was something they enjoyed far more than drug pushing. Sure, it provided more revenue, but aside from a few tense exchanges, it lacked the thrill of riding up to a boat and shooting at frightened seagoers. It was a power trip, and Ban-Jen relished every second of it.

"We only have two-thirds of a tank left," Anada said. He was seated near the outboard, hand on the throttle, his mohawk shifting in the breeze.

"That's all we really need," Ban-Jen replied. "We'll check out Coral Basin, then head back."

"You think those people know anything?" Kiet asked.

Ban-Jen shook his head. "Who cares?" He looked out past their stern. Two hundred feet behind them, the second skiff was also headed west. Though Goro wanted them checking different locations, their radios only seemed to work whenever they felt like it. Ban-Jen felt more comfortable with both teams remaining within eyesight.

"I think it's Chao Fah," Kiet said after a few minutes of silence. "It adds up. We sunk their boat the other day over the drop-off. He had to know it was us, so he retaliated."

Ban-Jen nodded. "I suspect that too. Plus, he's the only one who would send a message by doing what he did, shredding the docks like that and butchering our people."

"Yeah. They tore their arms off," Anada said. He was admiring his large, freshly sharpened machete. Every day, he ran a stone over the blade, making sure it was ready to cut through flesh and bone with ease. Often, he tested it on bamboo, sometimes hacking through thick stalks in just two whacks. He had run the stone over the blade this morning in hopes of encountering those responsible for the deaths of last night's watchers.

Ban-Jen stood up. "We're almost there."

The island was dead ahead, a half mile off their port bow. As they grew near, its inner details came into view, particularly the small valley in its center which connected to its west beach. On its southwest corner was a small peninsula that extended from the main body like a panhandle. It was covered in small, green vegetation, mainly long grass.

Ban-Jen was not thrilled about the idea of making landfall there, for if somebody was waiting, it would be too easy for them to hide in that long grass. At the same time, the west beach was way too wide open.

The best bet would be to circle the small island and see if any vessels were anchored nearby.

Understanding this as well, Kiet steered the boat to the south.

They were now near a quarter-mile from the island's panhandle when Ban-Jen snatched up his weapon with haste.

"What is that?"

Anada turned to look. "Where?"

Ban-Jen pointed to the shallows.

"I see it," Kiet exclaimed. "It's…" He angled his head, eyebrows raised. "Is that a boat?"

"A sunken boat," Anada said, now seeing it for himself.

They moved closer, the pirate on the bow pointing his weapon at the island's south shore in case any adversaries should appear.

The bow of the wreckage was slanted at an angle, the wheelhouse partially visible. Its overhead had been torn clean off, the hull bent out of proportion in various places.

"We don't have any guys out this way, do we?" Anada asked.

"No," Ban-Jen replied.

Kiet steered their skiff to the wreckage. Through the clear water, they could see the bottom where the stern was wedged. Its portside and aft deck were practically gone, the pieces scattered across the bottom. The silt coating the rocks and fragments appeared fresh and loose, only having settled recently.

Lying amongst the pieces was the dark frame of an automatic weapon. Ban-Jen looked long and hard, identifying the weapon as a Russian assault rifle.

None of Daow's arsenal included that brand of weapon. Most of what they currently had were looted from a Simolean pirate band sixteen months back.

"Let's turn around," he said. "We have our answer."

"Chao Fah?" Kiet asked.

"Gotta be. Bastard is choosing to go to war with us." Daow started to laugh. He knew Chao ran a small operation. Trying to take Daow head-on was suicide. But Chao Fah, unlike Daow, liked to get high on his own supply, obviously compromising his judgement.

His delight at the prospect of a firefight drifted away as their skiff turned west.

"Where are the others?"

Kiet and Anada sat straight, taking notice of the sudden absence of the second scout team.

The ocean in front of them was empty, save for a few brown flecks of wood fanning out.

Kiet slowed the boat, identifying those pieces as parts of the skiff.

Ban-Jen had his rifle shouldered. There was nobody in sight; no vessel or aircraft. It was as if the boat had simply imploded.

"A whale?" Kiet asked.

"I don't know."

The water rippled, rocking their skiff to and fro.

Ban-Jen pivoted to the left, rifle aimed low. Something passed under them. Something red. Something *huge*.

He turned in the opposite direction, just in time to see the thing circling back. It moved with the speed of an express train, its main body large and bulky, with large fins extending from its tip. On the opposite end was a group of long, thin extensions.

Limbs.

Tentacles.

"What the fu—"

The water exploded. Mist struck Ban-Jen in the eyes. He fired blindly, shouting in fright.

Anada screamed, his voice not coming from Ban-Jen's right, but *above* him. The pirate opened his eyes and watched as Anada kicked in midair. Coiled around him like a python was a blood-red tentacle, claws expanding from their disk-shaped suction cups, tearing into Anada's flesh.

Kiet was next to scream.

The club-shaped end of a titanic limb slapped down on his shoulder, driving him forward. His hands flung forward, grazing Ban-Jen with the blade of his prized machete before its tip plunged an inch into the bow of their skiff.

He lifted his head, eyes wide, yelling maniacally as curved hooks cut into his shoulder blade. Blood oozed from his flesh and drizzled onto the deck, some of it splattering Ban-Jen's face as Kiet was yanked from his seat into the water.

Anada, crushed like a grape, was next to disappear.

Ban-Jen was alone, lost to madness, watching the skiff break apart under him. The arms constricted it, cracking the hull and snapping it apart like a dead leaf.

The deck under his feet split, dropping Ban-Jen into the water.

He sank five feet, spinning a few times in the suction caused by the lashing of arms. He threw his hands out and stopped the spinning.

Two red eyes stared back at them, almost blending in to the huge, rubbery mass they were part of. From beneath those eyes came a red cloud where Anada and Kiet had been crushed into pulp—the same fate which awaited Ban-Jen.

The beast seized him and dragged him to its beak, shredding his flesh with its razor-lined tongue.

When it was all over, the creature ejected water from its siphon and headed west, leaving the wreckage of their small boat drifting to shore.

CHAPTER 9

The *Kingsford* anchored fifteen yards out from the southeast docks, the pirate horde on deck waiting for the skiffs to collect them and their prisoners.

Tracie put a hand on her son's shoulders, doing her best to keep herself from succumbing to the horror of their situation. In her mind, this was the sort of thing that only happened in old swashbuckling movies, not to *her*. And certainly not to Jon.

"Keep quiet," Ernie whispered to them. "Any resistance will only make things worse. Let's just hope they plan to hold us to ransom."

Rifle muzzles goaded their backs, pushing them forward. Tracie and Jon went first, climbing over the side onto the skiff awaiting them. Ernie was next, his first mate hesitant to join them on the ride to doom. A strike on the back of his neck by Goro brought Oliver to his knees.

The message was loud and clear: die on land, or dic right here on the boat. Naturally, the fisherman chose to extend his life as much as possible, even if there was nothing in his future but pain.

A small group of pirates awaited on shore, many of them making lewd gestures at their female prisoner. It was the most joy they would get—that, and maybe the opportunity to watch—as any action involving her was reserved for Daow.

Tracie set foot on the dock, holding Jon's hand. She walked past four pirates armed with AK-47s, all chattering amongst themselves as they watched her. Ernie was a few steps behind her, stumbling forward a couple of times after getting struck by one of those ushering him. There was no reason for them to do it other than the plain and simple joy.

Oliver was last in line, cursing, feeling Goro's rifle at his back.

They walked over a dirt trail that was as white-tan as the most soothing beaches. Rook Island, had it not been for its ugly population, would have otherwise been a thing of beauty.

As they traveled inland past lush green trees and bushes, they detected sounds from its interior. They were mechanical noises. Industrial.

Tracie slowed and leaned back towards Ernie, whispering, "What is that?"

"There's a petroleum plant here," he whispered. "Maybe they took it over."

"If they did, wouldn't there be a bunch of choppers around? Obviously, somebody would be monitoring the place."

Ernie listened to the sounds. It certainly did not sound like the plant was out of commission. If anything, it sounded perfectly operational.

"True."

"Talk again, and I will rip your teeth out," Goro warned. For good measure, he put his boot in Oliver's ass.

"Hey!" the fisherman yelled. "What did I—"

It wasn't often one got to see the inside of a gun barrel. Today was a first for Oliver. He moved away, the round piece of steel that was Goro's rifle muzzle burnt forever into his brain.

The settlement was a quarter mile inward. It was a large clearing, not by natural formation, but industrial excavation. The trees had been torn away and the ground flattened.

Several shacks had been erected on the northwest and southeast ends of the camp. At its rear was a large steel structure, almost shaped like a radio tower, operated by a skeleton crew of company employees who clearly had no issue with what was going on around them. To its right were four large white containers. On each of them was a yellow diamond label with symbols of multiple different languages. Among them was H2S.

"What is that?" Jon whispered.

"Hydrogen sulfide," his mother replied. "They had to remove it from the oil deposit. Can't just let it fly, because it's extremely deadly."

They heard Goro increasing his pace. He stopped in front of the line of prisoners and used aggressive hand motions to organize them into a row.

Standing side-by-side, they made eye contact with the head of this pirate encampment. With that red eye, he was the only one on this island more intimidating than Goro. He had a wooden table in front of him, with several knives laid out for the prisoners to see.

To the right of that table was a roaring campfire with a pully system nearby, its rope swinging high above the flames.

There was a man in a white shirt standing near the pirate leader. Those business casual clothes he wore made it damn clear he was not part of this gang; at least, not directly. Then again, maybe he was, since another man standing near him was also dressed in 'plain' clothes. Unlike the business guy, who looked extremely uncomfortable, the guy in the blue shirt with the button collar was just as upbeat as the rest of the clan.

The presence of opium plants and poppy seeds spelled out what the true revenue generator for this operation was. Not only that, it confirmed in Tracie's mind what had killed the shark and crabs in the drop-off.

Heroin.

Tracie looked at the businessman. *You piece of shit. You're helping these guys.*

"Is this all of them?" the leader asked Goro.

"It is. We have others searching for any other vessels."

The leader stood up from his chair.

Ernie juddered as though zapped by an electric fence.

"Oh, shit," he whispered through clenched teeth. "Daow Aree."

Tracie and Jon did not know who that was, but it did not matter. Common sense was enough for them to know this guy was bad news.

"Tell me your names," Daow said.

Ernie took the initiative. "Ernie, Oliver, Tracie, and Jon."

"And what is your business here?"

"Scientific research," Tracie said.

"We were out to find the ugliest creatures in the region," Jon said. "We can now report back that we have succeeded."

Tracie squeezed his hand, not affectionately, but in a 'shut up!' way.

Daow looked at Goro, then at the other pirates nearby. A few moments of tense silence followed. Then came hysterical laughter.

"I like him," Daow said. "He'll fit in well here." His eyes went to Tracie. "So would his mother."

Jon nudged forward, ready to trade blows with the fanatic. Goro put himself in his path, stopping him with a look powerful enough to crush brick.

Daow picked up one of his knives. "Before we can entertain those possibilities, I'm gonna need to press for some information. So, I'll start by asking the easy way: who are you really with?"

The four prisoners exchanged nervous glances.

"Nobody," Oliver said.

Daow spat some chewing tobacco into the fire. "That's what I thought." He pointed his blade in their direction, lining its tip with each prisoner counting "eenie-meenie-miney-moe."

The end of the little rhyme concluded with the knife pointing at Jon.

Tracie put herself in front of him. "No! Please!"

Jon put his hands on her arms and eased her to the side. He remembered what his father had explained while talking about a situation where one of his people were captured by the enemy.

They want to get under your skin. Don't give them any reaction.

"It'll be alright," he said to her.

Without saying anything else, he stepped forward. As he passed Goro, he decided he wanted one small taste of satisfaction.

The pirate brute was caught off guard by the punch to the chin.

Once again, Daow and the rest of the camp laughed. It took a few moments for Goro to overcome his killer instinct and join in.

Two other men approached and took Jon by the arms, binding his wrists behind his back before swinging the pulley over.

"You've got spirit, boy," Daow said. "That's actually why I chose you. I mean, hell, will anyone care if I hung the slob or his first mate? Nah, I'd rather throw them in the pit with bugs over behind them bushes over there." He pointed his knife southwest. "One thing at a time. Let's see how long that spirit of yours will last."

***

"I see the boat," Hatcher said. "Hopefully we're not too late."

Kane kept low on the aft deck with him and Taft, waiting for Agent Ravee to line the *Grand Voyager* up with the dock. To their right was the *Saint Nicholas*, with Axel at the helm, wearing a brown jacket belonging to one of the original crewmembers. He kept his face down, making sure not to be noticed by the four pirates waiting at the dock.

They shouted at Ravee in Thai, their tones unfriendly.

The boat came to a stop.

Kane waited a few more seconds. He was glad he did, as three other pirates came jogging down the trail in their direction.

"Team Two, you set?"

"Ready to go," Vladik whispered.

"Three…two…one… GO!"

At once, the mercenaries emerged from hiding. Silenced gunfire delivered a devastating wave of bullets. In a count of four, all seven targets had their center mass cut open. Without even squeezing off a return shot, they hit the ground.

Kane was the first to set foot on land. He moved forward, providing cover while the rest of the team disembarked.

Footsteps and confused voices alerted him to approaching hostiles on his left. He pivoted and took aim, surprising both pirates with headshots.

"Quit hogging them all," Taft quipped.

Agent Ravee, holding a HK 416, joined Kane at the front of the group.

"Camp's up that way," he said, prodding his weapon at the trail.

"From what I can see, almost all of the pirates are gathered up there," Woodley said. "Prisoners too."

"They don't have much time." Kane twirled his finger at his men, instructing them to huddle. Woodley held out his tablet, displaying a zoomed image of the encampment. "They're about to torture one of them. There's three guys around the fire. Hatcher, take position on the southeast corner near those trees. Looks like there's a little bit of elevation right there, and enough cover to keep you out of sight. Woodley, Axel, work your way around this white structure here… Agent, you know what those are? They look like storage tanks."

"Probably containers for hydrogen sulfide," Ravee answered.

"Oh, great," Kane muttered. "Keep that in mind while shooting these guys—*don't* hit the tanks." He looked at Vladik and Taft. "You guy are with me. Hatcher, you have the Shooting Star?"

Hatcher proudly sported the guided missile launcher strapped over his back.

"Affirmative, boss."

"It might come in handy if they try to make a run to the northwest dock. Do not use it in the camp."

"Aw. Well, I guess I can hold off," the sniper retorted.

Kane loaded a fresh magazine into his weapon and sprung into action.

"Stay off the trail. Let's go."

***

Jon squirmed like an inchworm on the ground, his feet tied together with rope and secured to a hook at the end of the pully. The pirate operating the device hoisted him off the ground, maintaining a three-foot gap between his head and the dirt underneath him.

Twisting and turning from the end of the line, he felt like a fish that had been hooked by its tailfin and lifted out of the water.

Daow stood near the fire, dipping his knife into the hot coals.

Tracie could barely stand up. This was any parent's worst nightmare. Twice, she pleaded with the pirate that she did not know anything. All it seemed to do was make him drag this out even more.

He pulled the knife from the flame, admiring its red-hot tip. As he moved to Jon, it was clear what he had in mind.

Tracie did not care what the guy wanted. All she cared about was freeing her son from this hell.

“Okay, we’re with someone,” she said.

Daow paused, waiting for her to follow up on that statement.

Tracie panted, having no details to support her lie. “We… we’re with… the agency… the Central—”

“Stop,” Oliver growled. “He’s gonna know you’re lying, and that’s only gonna make it worse.” He immediately cringed, realizing he did that himself by stopping her.

“Oh!” Daow said. “So, not only did you lie about not being involved with any agency, now you’re lying about *which* agency you’re with. Maybe this’ll motivate you.”

The pirate leaned forward and extended the blade to Jon’s left cheek.

He groaned, muscles tensing as the searing hot tip grazed the flesh under his eye down to his chin.

Daow withdrew the blade and took joy in the fresh scar. “Around here, that’s a badge of honor!”

“Fuck you,” Jon replied.

“Let him go,” Tracie said. “He did nothing to deserve this.”

“Only one way to find out,” Daow said. He toyed with the knife, thinking of giving his prisoner another scar.

“Do it,” Jon said.

Tracie held her breath. It was the strangest sensation she had ever experienced. Behind the terror she felt, there was a hint of pride. She could see her husband, Brandon, speaking through her son.

Never did she realize Jon was so brave. He truly was following in Brandon's footsteps.

The pirate lit a cigarette with his freshly heated knife. During his first draw on it, he watched Jon, contemplating on what to do next.

"I've had people talk tough to me before." He backed away and returned to his seat near the table of knives. "It's usually not long before they're singing a new tune. Let's see how long you last." He clicked his tongue at the men near the pulley. "Put him over the fire."

Tracie was back to being utterly terrified.

"No!"

Jon cursed at the men as they sniggered at one another. One of them stepped behind the pulley and grabbed a handle, slowly swinging him over the flames.

A strange whistle streaked through the air.

In that same moment, the man at the pulley's handle jolted, blood shooting from his chest and back.

Two more whistles streaked immediately after, the other pirates at the pulley reeling backwards with their chests blown open.

Everyone went quiet.

Daow rose from his seat, his mind registering what he had just witnessed.

"What…"

By the time he realized what was going on, it was too late.

"Showtime."

Kane emerged from cover alongside Ravee, popping off rounds in quick succession. The pirates near the three standing hostages shuddered, both from the shock of their enemy's arrival and the physical tremor of having lead cut through their bodies.

Like bowling pins, they collapsed around the hostages.

More gunfire ripped from the northeast side as Woodley and Axel stormed the camp, creating a crossfire the enemy forces could not escape.

The pirate leader, Daow, had shed his skin of violent confidence and was retreating from his sacrificial ritual, leaving his men to do the fighting.

Taft and Vladik joined their commander in the assault, vaulting grenades into the western part of the camp.

A series of earth-shattering explosions shook the ground and kicked up dust, throwing the pirate horde into further confusion and mismanagement.

Some of them returned fire, unable to keep up with the movements of their intruders.

Ravee moved over to the hostages, instructing them to move back to a safe position while the fighting resumed.

"Get Jon!" the woman said.

The young man shook upside-down from the rope, adding enthusiasm to her point.

"Yeah, I'd really appreciate it!"

Kane took the initiative and ran to the pulley. With Ravee's help, he pulled the teenager named Jon away from the fire and lowered him to the ground.

Taft moved inward, gunning down a pair of pirates who were coming at his commander and the hostage. They spun in place after absorbing the bullets, ultimately faceplanting in the dirt.

Kane freed Jon's legs and wrists. The kid separated his hands and arose, not without giving the mercenary his thanks.

"You injured?" Kane asked him.

"I'm good."

"Good. Now get with your mother and… whoa! What are ya doing?"

Jon picked one of the AK-47s from the dead pirates, flipped it over to properly grip it, and fired a burst of rounds at some pirates bunching up near one of the shacks.

One of them caught a round in the thigh, dropping him.

Kane analyzed the situation. There were at least eight pirates gathered near the shacks on the left side of the camp, using them as cover while they attempted to repel the mercs.

Several more were climbing up onto the rig, taking firing positions on its platforms to use its height to their advantage.

"Hatcher, eyes up."

"I see them, boss."

Kane heard the whistles from sniper rounds zipping across the camp. One of the pirates took a hit, blasting his AK-47 wildly as he tumbled off the rig.

Another one attempted to switch spots. He completed a total of two steps when Hatcher planted a round in his temple.

A third one attempted a Hail Mary, firing into all of the vegetation at the edge of camp. The entire layout, designed to keep their camp hidden from prying eyes, was now working against them.

Hatcher struck the hostile through the heart, the round passing out his back and into the throat of a fourth pirate behind him. Both of them tumbled off the platform and hit the dirt.

More bullets struck the ground near Kane's position. It was not just the pirates trying to gun them down, but the oil workers.

The dumbasses. All they needed to do was keep still and do nothing, and they would've been free to go. But no, they had to join in.

Whether Agent Ravee would go after any of the workers of the petroleum company was his prerogative. Kane's team was hired to eliminate Daow Aree. But not that these idiots, who were clearly handpicked by the corrupt executive and probably having backgrounds that were less than upstanding, were joining the fight, they were no different than the cutthroats they fought alongside.

Hatcher took one of them out with his sniper rifle.

The sight of one of their own going down gave the others pause. After looking at one another, they resumed shooting.

Hatcher sniped another one, the bullet hitting him with enough force to lift him off his feet.

Kane fired a few shots at the platform, dropping another one of the workers.

Realizing they were outgunned, the rest of the men in tattered white shirts began their retreat to ground level, where they started making a run to the northwest docks.

Seeing the direction in which they fled confirmed to Kane where Daow had retreated to. The pirate lord was trying to make a run for it, and Kane had no intention of letting him go.

First, he needed to exterminate a few remaining pests in his way.

He saw Axel and Woodley arriving near the east legs of the rig. Kane waved to them and signaled for them to provide cover fire while he advanced to the shacks.

A wave of ammunition forced the pirates into hiding.

Kane made his run.

He arrived at the first shack, caught a glimpse of movement through the window, and tossed a grenade.

Tucking his head down, he felt the resulting *BOOM* and heard the "WAAH" of the lowlife inside. When the commander looked again, the hostile was plastered against the wall.

He moved to the next shack, firing through the window at a pirate who was responding to the grenade explosion. His head whipped back, struck dead center by a single shot from Kane's rifle.

There was a second pirate inside that building. He was attempting to return fire against Axel and Woodley when he realized his companion was dead. He turned to shoot at Kane, but was beaten to the draw. Three rounds punched through his chest, knocking him against the sink with a very undignified look on his face.

Farther down the line of shacks, two pirates attempted to make a run for it. One of them was dropped by Hatcher. The second one was intercepted by Taft, who moved left of the buildings.

"I got a visual on a couple heading northwest," he called to Kane.

"That's where Daow's headed," the commander replied.

He checked his surroundings, spinning to the left when he saw two men seemingly appear out of nowhere. They were both unarmed and raising their hands, the guy in the white shirt shouting, "Don't shoot! I give up!" The guy next to him, wearing a blue shirt, raised his hands as well, though he exhibited anger as opposed to the white-shirt's trepidation.

Ravee and Vladik moved in on the two men, checked them for weapons, and placed them in restraints.

With them secured, Kane turned around to resume the fight. Axel and Woodley were exchanging gunfire with some guys near the last shack, Taft was hooking around the left to flank them… all the while, a pirate emerged from around the corner and pointed a handgun in the commander's face.

Kane reacted with a swing of his rifle, smacking the gun out of the enemy's hand. The pirate retaliated with impressively fast speed, performing a three-hundred-and-sixty-degree turn, launching a spinning kick which connected with Kane's H&K.

Literally empty-handed, the commander decided to deal with the bastard one-on-one.

The pirate, yelling in an effort to spark fear, threw another lightning-fast kick. Kane thrust his arm to the left, his fist hammering the guy's foot and redirecting it. For the second time, the pirate attempted a three-sixty-degree spin kick. Before he could get his foot off the ground, Kane moved in and conked him in the face with an elbow.

The pirate hit the ground, spitting blood and showing a depletion in confidence, but unwilling to quit. He got back on his feet, took a few steps back, and with a yell, charged at the commander.

He sprang from the ground in a bounding leap, extending his foot out with enough force to smash a two-by-four.

Kane shifted to the left, letting his opponent miss entirely. After the pirate touched down, he threw a kick of his own. The pirate grunted from the intense impact and fell head over heels… ultimately ending up in the campfire.

"AGH! AAAAGH!"

His clothes lit up as though soaked with gasoline. Given the rig he was working near, that probably was not out of the realm of possibility. Like a burning starfish, he floundered with all four limbs sticking outward, his flesh sizzling like bacon in a greased pan.

Kane reclaimed his weapon and ran northwest, linking up with Axel, Woodley, and Taft.

Hatcher emerged from cover and joined them, discarding his sniper rifle in favor of his submachine gun.

They followed a trail similar to the one that connected the camp to the southeast dock.

Midway down, they encountered a pair of pirates. Dedicated to their leader's survival, they stood their ground and sprayed bullets at the mercs.

Kane took out the one on the left, Taft blasting the one on the right.

They proceeded toward the dock.

It was larger than the southeast one, having been designed for the petroleum company's boats. Three vessels were in the middle of departing, all forty-foot cruisers.

Standing on the aft deck of the center vessel was Daow, taunting the mercenaries with a crude gesture.

"He really thinks he looks good in this situation, doesn't he?" Taft remarked.

"Give it thirty more seconds," Kane replied. "Trust me, he won't be laughing."

They converged on the dock. There, four armed drillers were in the middle of boarding a small company vessel. One of them looked over at the team, his hand reaching for his rifle which lay atop of a fuel drum.

"Don't do it," Kane warned.

The guy did it, and took a round to the face as a result.

His three companions attempted a last stand, only to be wiped out within two seconds by precise shooting.

Kane and his men gathered at the pier. The boats were forty meters out and gaining distance.

He got into the company boat with Axel, Woodley, and Taft.

Rifle fire echoed from the aft deck of all three boats as Daow's remaining forces attempted to deter any pursuit.

"Hatcher, now you can put your toy to use," Kane said.

"With pleasure."

Hatcher placed his submachine gun down and unslung the Shooting Star. He put his eye to the digital scope and zoomed in on the vessel to the left of Daow's. The men on board were still emptying their rifles, hoping to land a lucky shot.

The computer locked on to their heat signature.

Hatcher deployed the rocket.

In a span of a second, it traveled from the launcher, over the sea, smack dab into the vessel. The deck erupted, the blast igniting the fuel and triggering a secondary explosion all in a split second.

As Kane predicted, Daow's confidence vanished in the blink of an eye.

"Get the other one."

"Don't need to tell me twice."

Hatcher reloaded the Shooting Star, locked onto the boat to Daow's right, and fired.

The rocket struck the vessel square in the middle, sending pirates hurtling through the air. Burning debris went skyward like fireworks, trailing thin grey smoke. The vessel split in half and quickly plunged into the sea.

Kane got on the company boat's radio and spoke into the mic. "Stop engines now, drop all weapons overboard, or you're next, shithead."

They could hear the pirate lord cursing as the engine switched off. The handful of pirates on board with him tossed their guns in the water, determined not to share the explosive fate of their comrades.

Kane put his hand on the throttle, glancing at Hatcher before taking off. "They do anything stupid, 'blast em."

"Just don't target us by mistake!" Taft added.

"I'll try not to," Hatcher retorted.

"You all are cowards!" Daow shouted at his men. "You are failures! I may as well have hired women!"

"Look at what they have done!" one of his men said, holding his hand out to the burning wreckage on their starboard side. "Doing nothing means we end up like that!"

"We'll end up that way anyway," Daow replied. He watched as the commando unit approached with the company boat. The satisfied look on one of their faces, knowing he had secured victory, pissed the pirate lord off even more. "Fuck it!"

He went into the cabin and came right back out, holding a rifle he had found inside. Shouldering the weapon, he squeezed the trigger.

His subordinate grabbed the barrel and shifted it downward, directing the bullets into the water.

Daow struck the man across the face. "What are you doing?!"

"I don't want to get blown up!"

Daow pointed the rifle at him. If there was even a tiny bit of solace to be had, it would be from punishing those he considered traitors.

BAM!

The boat rocked heavily, throwing the four men on the aft deck off balance.

"What was that?" one of them said.

They heard a yell and a splash somewhere near the bow.

Right away, there was another splash, followed by a squeal from someone up on the bridge.

Daow climbed the ladder and laid eyes on the flying bridge. It was empty, save for a small puddle of seawater.

The boat rocked again.

Now, it was the men on the aft deck screaming.

Daow stood up and looked down.

What he saw—what he *thought* he saw—was a huge red cloud beneath the vessel. In the moments that followed, he realized it was not a cloud, but a living entity whose size dwarfed that of the boat it stalked.

It looked truly otherworldly in its body shape and mass. When it came to the way it stared back up at him, it was more than alien—it was the devil himself.

In a rare instance, Daow Aree was truly dumbstruck.

"My god…"

Those arms rose from the water like hungry serpents, lashing at the boat and those on board.

"Holy mother of ass!" Taft exclaimed.

"Boss, are you seeing this?" Hatcher said.

Kane did in fact see it, and he could not believe what was in front of his eyes. There were four of the worm-shaped leviathans, their suction cups and attack methods all at once familiar and foreign.

Tentacles.

Nearing their target, they got a visual on the main body where all of those deadly arms met together. It was arrow-shaped with a length surpassing that of the vessel it tore apart.

"It's a goddamn squid."

"A *giant* squid," Taft added. It was a species he had heard of before, but he never knew the 'giant' part to be so literal.

One after another, the pirates were snatched from the aft deck. The beast shifted its position, putting itself on the starboard side. Two of its arms lifted out of the water and bent like the letter Z. Like spears, they plowed through the hull and ripped outward.

More arms appeared on the boat's portside, shifting left, right, up, and down, wrecking everything inside.

On the flying bridge, Daow blasted his assault rifle. Of the thirty rounds he spewed, three of them managed to hit one of the arms.

The beast raised its head from the water, exposing eyes that were as red and raw as the meat it craved.

Detecting motion, the beast turned those eyes to the approaching vessel and the men in black aboard.

"Hatcher, can you get a lock on the thing?"

"Negative, sir. It has no heat signature. Can you use laser targeting?"

"Laser the target," Kane said to his men.

All four of them pointed their guns and connected their laser dots on the beast.

Their effort was cut short. Like a praying mantis, it lunged with its ten arms. The boat rocked to stern, throwing Taft and Woodley on their backs. Axel fired a few rounds, hitting one of the tentacles and sending it retreating under the sea.

Another one emerged in its place, smacking the mercenary across the chest, knocking him down.

Kane dropped to one knee, avoiding the swipe of a large tentacle with a clubbed tip. It passed over his head and disappeared into the water.

Using the Shooting Star was a no-go; not without blowing themselves up in the process. Rifle fire wasn't going to cut it either. They would be in the water before they could inflict any significant damage.

They needed a new weapon; something quick, available, and capable of widespread damage.

He looked at the aft deck. Near the fallen Taft was a black fuel drum.

"Open that thing up and get it into the water!" he said.

Seeing what he was pointing at, Woodley and Axel pushed Taft aside, unscrewed the cap, and lifted the drum over the side.

Kane engaged the throttle and cut the wheel to port, turning the boat around. The guys behind him dumped the fuel, coating the water above the kraken's head with diesel.

They pushed more, throwing the entire drum overboard. Rifle fire bombarded the thing, piercing its sides with fierce impacts. Sparks flew, expanding into a blanket of roaring flames.

Axel pumped a fist. "Yeah!"

The tentacles whipped about with urgency, their flesh baking in the literal sea of fire.

In one fluid motion, the arms slipped into the ocean. Kane looked to the south, watching a streak of red pass under the waves.

"What the hell was THAT?" Agent Ravee exclaimed.

He, Vladik, and the hostages had gathered at the dock, all having witnessed the spectacular event.

"Something I don't want to see again," Kane replied. "Berkley, you reading me?"

"Loud and clear, boss. Everything go as planned?"

"More or less. Bring the chopper to Rook Island. We're gonna need an airlift. Trust me, we *do not* want to travel by water."

"Roger that. On my way."

Kane took a long, deep breath. The mission was almost over. It was a weird one, especially after what they had just encountered, but unless that monster squid learned how to fly, they would soon be out of here.

First thing's first; they had to collect their target. He was huddled on the bridge of his sinking boat, baring teeth in fear and humiliation.

"Agent Ravee, prepare for delivery of your prisoner."

CHAPTER 10

The shooting had stopped and the screams had gone silent. Tremors from heavy artillery blasts had shaken the west side of the island, claiming the last few members of the pirate clan.

Goro huddled thirty meters from camp, concealing himself with the island's flora. It was rare he ever felt humiliated, and ever more rare that he was bested in a fight.

He did not partake much in the recent firefight. The grenades thrown by the attack force at the start of the raid had literally sent him flying. By simple miracle, he only received one shrapnel wound. The shockwave was a little less forgiving, having rattled his senses well enough to leave him on the ground, stunned.

In a way, it was a stroke of luck in itself, for the commandos bypassed him, believing him to be dead.

They were out of sight at the moment. From the sounds of it, they had gathered at the northwest dock. There was no way for him to know whether or not Daow was alive; not without getting a visual of the enemy.

Goro was loyal. Extremely loyal. But only to a point. If Daow was dead, there was no use in making a move on the enemy. He was outnumbered and outgunned. In that scenario, it was preferable to stay hidden and wait for the infiltrators to depart.

Afterwards, he would take a boat, flee the island, and make a new life for himself.

On the other hand, if Daow was alive, then there would be cause for Goro to take action. He would need to be strategic. Going in guns blazing would only result in his leader's death in addition to his own. He would have to hit the enemy where it hurt. It was a plan without a plan. In other words, Goro needed to improvise.

He checked his weapon. A full magazine was loaded in his rifle. His pistol had slipped out of its holster during the madness. There were plenty of other weapons to choose from, but they were all in the camp, in plain view. Going to get one would be suicide, for the enemy group was presently heading back that way.

Goro thought fast, deciding his best course of action would be to take position between the two locations the commandos would gather. Either they would use a boat from the southeast dock or gather near the south beach, which was spacious enough for a chopper to land.

Considering the fact they were well supplied and used the *Grand Voyager* and *Saint Nicholas* to get here, he assumed they would depart by chopper.

Hearing their movements and voices, he kept low and approached the south shore, ultimately finding a place where he could remain hidden while observing his enemy.

***

Daow Aree made sure to stick his tongue out at Agent Ravee. It was a childish gesture, yet disturbing in its own right.

The agent breathed through his nose in an effort to compose himself. In the end, he decided composure was overrated and he clocked the pirate in the chin.

"Woah!" Daow laughed, spitting blood. "That's how you greet an old friend?"

"Old friend, my ass," Ravee said. "You know what you've done? You know what? Don't answer that."

The pirate sported a red grin. "Okay, I won't."

"Good, because you'd delight in the answer." Ravee raised another fist, tempted for a second go at his chin, but held back. "I personally know two people who've overdosed on your drugs. Up until eighteen months ago, my island had no issues with narcotics. We lived in peace, went to work, got married, had kids."

"You mean 'we' as a general statement, or did you marry one of these guys?" Daow said, waving his finger at the mercs.

Ravee punched him again.

"Oooookay." Hatcher put his hands on the agent and pulled him away from their prisoner. "Let's dial it back a notch."

"My point is we were flourishing, both in our culture and economically. Then your poison came to our shores and ruined everything. Now, we're an embarrassment to many of our mainland neighbors, who look at us as an island of drug addicts."

"Aren't they dealing with the same problem?" Taft asked.

"Yes, but they have enough media influence to downplay the problem," Ravee explained.

Kane raised a hand, putting an end to this topic. "Listen, it's done. We got him. It's over. You get to take him home and lock him up indefinitely. As for now, I just want to get out of here." He tapped his mic. "Berkley, what's your ETA?"

"Five minutes."

"Suits me."

"I'd advise directing him to the south shore," Ravee said. "It'll be easier for him to set down and pick us all up."

"Got it. Berkley, bring the chopper to the south beach and set her down. We've got more than a few passengers to get out of here."

"Copy that."

They trekked across the island, cutting through the camp where they had wiped out Daow's forces. It was a nice way of rubbing it in, especially for Ravee, who wanted the pirate to suffer for his atrocities.

As they walked, Kane took a moment to check on the teenager, Jon. When bringing the prisoner to shore, he had gotten the pleasure of learning the names of the four civilians.

Jon was still holding the AK-47, resembling a soldier in Vietnam who had taken the weapon of an enemy combatant.

"You alright there, *Colonel?*" he quipped.

Jon smiled. "No way would I want to be a colonel. I want to actually do some real work."

"Ah! For what it's worth, you seem cut out for the job." He looked past his new ally at Tracie. "You okay, ma'am? Haven't had the chance to ask, you know, with battling evil pirates and giant squids."

"Hazards of the job, right?" she joked. "Yes, I'm good. Thanks to all of you. Your timing was perfect."

"We're good like that," Taft chimed in, bouncing on his toes.

"We were lucky," Kane said modestly. "Both with getting here on time *and* avoiding becoming the special of the day."

"Right?" Hatcher jogged to speak with Tracie. "So, you're a scientist?"

"Correct."

"What was that thing?"

"It is what you think it is," she replied. "*Architeuthis Dux.* Simply put, a giant squid."

Taft scoffed. "Yeah, giant alright. I didn't know they got that big."

"I didn't either," Tracie said. "Most specimens don't have a mantle length more than eighteen feet. That one is truly gargantuan."

"Where'd it come from?" Rudy, the oil executive asked. Even with decades of imprisonment ahead of him, all he could currently focus on were those monster tentacles.

"If I had to venture a theory, I'd say it resided in the trench a few miles south of here, beyond the drop-off," she explained. "For all of its life, it hunted and fed, growing and growing, with no reason to come to the surface."

"Until now," Taft said. "Why now? What's got that thing so riled up that it wants to attack anything that floats?"

"That's my second theory," Tracie said. "I believe your friend here..." She pointed her elbow at Daow, "...had an accident of sorts. He dumped a ship-full of heroin into the trench. The squid, among other deep-sea animals, gorged on the drug. Many of them could not handle the side effects and died. Squids are believed to have advanced immune systems, which would explain why it survived. But, it didn't get off scot-free—it's addicted, and it's gonna go after any vessel it can find in hopes of getting its next fix."

"Oh, that's wonderful," Axel remarked. "A heroin-addicted sea monster. Now I've seen everything."

Ravee took the opportunity to punish Daow once more with a smack on the head. "You've been dumping drugs into the ocean? Why?"

"I've done no such thing," the pirate shot back.

"It wasn't so much dumped," Tracie said. "More like, a boat had recently sunk and the sea life infiltrated its cargo hold."

"So, *Captain Sparrow* lost a boat?" Taft asked.

"I have not," Daow said with pride. "I only attacked a rival shipper who passed through my territory. I guess you Westerners would call him a mule."

The group stopped.

"Wait, there's someone else out here cooking up drugs?" Ravee asked.

"Chao Fah," the pirate answered. For once, he was glad to cooperate. Even in the wake of his own downfall, he did not want to see any of his competitors succeed.

"Eh." Ravee kept walking. "I know his name. I thought he fled into the mainland. At least we know he's out here too. Chao Fah's a small fry. Bringing him down should be even easier than Aree."

The pirate spat at the back of his neck.

"One thing at a time," Kane said.

They arrived at the south beach and admired the late morning sunshine and the salty breeze coming off the ocean.

"We're at the beach, Berkley. Waiting on you," Kane said.

"What's the rush, boss? Got a date?"

"Yeah, with a case of beer at home."

"Sounds like a match made in heaven. I'm coming around now."

As soon as those words were spoken, the chopper emerged from the east. It hooked around, descending to twenty feet over the waves.

The team spread out, giving Berkley space to set down.

A heavy gust swept the shore, kicking up dust and shaking the leaves of nearby trees.

Jon and Tracie joined together in a hug. In sixty seconds, they would be on their way home.

***

Goro watched between the large green leaves of the bush concealing him from danger. He could see the enemy squad waiting at the shore with the people he had captured from the boat. In addition to them was Eiji and Rudy, both silent as the grave while they awaited their fate.

Goro could not have cared less about them. The third prisoner, however, was someone worth sticking his neck out for.

Daow Aree was alive and in good condition.

The downdraft from the approaching chopper came down hard on the island and traveled across the nearby area, further masking his appearance.

He needed to act now. The bird was a few feet away from touching down. Once they had Daow aboard, there would be no getting him out.

Goro extended his rifle through the barrier of vegetation, took aim at the cockpit, and opened fire.

***

CLANG! CLANG! CLANG!

The sound of bullets striking the hull accompanied by cracks of gunfire forced the team to duck for cover.

"Holy shit!"

Taking hits near his window, Berkley pulled up and retreated over the ocean.

The shooting persisted, with several of those bullets striking the aircraft's portside. Berkley banked hard to starboard, nearly spinning out of control. The chopper took a dive, its underbelly and tail rotor grazing the water's surface.

Tracie covered her mouth. "Oh, God!"

"There!" Jon shouted, pointing west of their position.

Kane saw it too; an AK-47 held and operated by a gorilla of a human being.

"Son of a bitch! Goro's still alive."

The commander returned fire. Goro ducked for cover, dropping his rifle in the process.

Kane broke into a sprint. "I'm going after him. Get on that chopper!"

"I'm coming with you, boss!" Taft called out.

Kane wasn't going to argue.

He passed over the spot where Goro had watched them, finding the trail left in his wake.

"Damn," Taft said. "You literally shot the gun out of his hand."

"Glad you're impressed," Kane replied.

He followed the trail fifteen degrees to his right, coming across a patch of jungle.

Immediately, he felt uncomfortable standing in this small opening surrounded by trees and bushes.

If he was on the run and wanted to ambush his pursuers, this would be the spot.

A shift of motion on his left made Kane pivot. Goro came at him, swinging a heavy branch like a baseball bat. The H&K was knocked from his grip. A second swing caught him on the helmet, knocking him to the ground.

"Whoa!" Taft lined up with the threat and took aim.

Like a primitive warrior, Goro put the branch over his shoulder and launched it as though spearing a fish. The end of the branch struck Taft right between the eyes, knocking him backwards.

Kane was back on his feet, his head drumming from the blow. He reached for his pistol and lifted it from its holster. Before he could extend it in the proper direction, a large hand with a mighty grip closed over his wrist, stopping him in place.

Kane struggled, sensing the superior strength of the pirate overwhelming him. Shooting the guy was impossible. Holding on to the pistol would only assure Goro would pry the weapon from his grip and use it against him.

Shifting his body weight to the right, he let the gun fling into the grass, instead opting to kick the pirate in the knees.

The impacts hurt, evidenced by the loosening of Goro's hold on the commander. A headbutt followed, landing with extra force thanks to the helmet.

Kane shook his arm free and went to throw a punch.

His fist was stopped midair by Goro's hand.

It was an uncomfortable feeling for the mercenary, enhanced by the sinister look on the pirate's face.

A right uppercut connected with Kane's chin, literally lifting him off the ground. Next thing he knew, he was in the grass, envisioning stars circling his head like in a cartoon.

He rolled to his feet and took a fighting stance, bracing for the pirate's next attack.

***

For a moment, it seemed as if the chopper would smash into the sea. Jon breathed in a much-needed sigh of relief when its pilot regained control. It held in position, literally a foot or two above the water.

"Talk about a rush," the pilot said through the comms. *"Take two. Hopefully, this time will be without surprises."*

SPLASH!

"Oh, shit!" Axel shouted.

The tentacles rose from the water with frightening speed, lassoing its tail. Berkley pulled up, gaining only a few feet of altitude before the arms resisted. Their immense strength overpowered that of the Blackhawk, dragging it down.

Alarms blared from inside the cockpit.

The chopper rocked side to side, the engines whining in protest.

Underneath, the squid unleashed more of its arms, its horrible face peering through the surface.

"Holy dear God!"

He banked to starboard, inadvertently putting the chopper into a spin.

The tail rotors caught one of the tentacles, severing it near its tip. Blue blood jetted from the stump, the beast spasming from sudden pain. Tentacles lashed upward, striking the chopper's underside.

Now in a true tailspin, the chopper spiraled inland. Berkley could be heard through the comms, cursing and praying to God to let him stop the out-of-control bird.

"Oh, no, no, no," Hatcher muttered, watching their ride fishtailing to the north. Even worse was the rapid descent as all control was truly lost.

The group raced inland, stopping after hearing the deafening crash inside of the pirate camp. A fireball rose over the trees, confirming Berkley's death as well as the destruction of their ride and the rig.

A gust of hot air swept over the group.

Woodley sniffed. "What's that smell?"

Tracie perked up. "Oh, no…"

"Rotten eggs?" Axel asked.

"That's hydrogen sulfide," she said. "The gas has been released."

"Oh, SHIT!" Hatcher exclaimed. "The crash ruptured the tanks. That stuff is gonna be all over the island in a matter of minutes. We need to get out of here or we're dead."
"Where should we go?" Oliver asked.

"No choice," Ernie replied. "We have to take the boats."

"The *Saint Nicholas* is low on fuel, and we don't have time to replenish it," Vladik said.

"Same with the *Grand Voyager*," Hatcher replied.

"Then we take my boat," Ernie said. "Take the skiffs to it and climb aboard!"

"What about the squid?" Rudy cried.

"Oh, right," Jon said. "Maybe you'd rather stay here."

The disgraced executive looked in the direction of the fire. "Nah, boat's fine."

As they made their evacuation, Hatcher went west. Nobody needed to ask where he was going. The answer was obvious: he needed to get Kane.

***

The commander dropped to one knee, his brain feeling as if it was juddering inside his skull. Every hit from the pirate was like kissing the express train.

Goro grabbed him by the shoulder and lifted Kane to his feet, smiling as he smashed him against a tree. A punch made contact to his stomach, folding him over.

He struck again, this time with a left hook.

Kane teetered to the side, his vision blurry. By now, the fight was nothing more than a game for his adversary. Goro was larger and stronger than he was. No man stood a chance against him. And those who thought they did, he gladly destroyed. Slowly. Painfully.

It was a mindset Kane was counting on.

Goro grabbed his chin and straightened him against the tree, pulling his fist back, ready to put it through the mercenary's face.

Exhaling like a bull, he put all of his power into it.

Kane tilted, the fist grazing his temple and smashing against the trunk of the tree.

Goro stumbled backward, holding his mangled hand. The knuckles had been smashed into the palm, the wrist bent out of shape, pieces of bark protruding from the skin.

Kane, pissed off, decided to get even.

He charged the pirate, pushing him backward through the jungle. His first punch landed on the ridge of Goro's nose. A second one went low, deliberately striking the pirate's broken hand. That sparked a shrieking reaction.

Kane threw a 'soccer kick' into the shin, dropping Goro to one knee. His next kick had more forward thrust to it, his heel connecting with Goro's chest.

The pirate tumbled backward, seemingly disappearing through the ground.

Kane, catching his breath, approached the large pit where his enemy had fallen into.

Goro lay on his back, half-conscious. Sudden pain snapped him back into reality.

He looked down at himself, then babbled frantically. Converging on him was a horde of ugly insects.

Kane had no idea what species they were, but one thing was for sure: they liked to eat flesh.

Goro kicked and squirmed, blood dripping from his chest, neck, and arms. In a matter of seconds, he was completely covered by the little brown bodies. A few seconds later, rivers of blood appeared through the swarming mass.

Kane inhaled, relieved to have actually managed to best the mountain of a man. In that breath, he detected the smell of rotten eggs.

Alarm bells went off in his head.

During the fight, he heard the crash, but was too busy to think anything of it.

"Commander!" Hatcher called from the east.

"I'm here!"

Hatcher moved to the sound of his voice. "Ah, there you are. Thank God. We gotta move."

"What happened?"

"The damn squid!" Hatcher shouted, his voice deep in anger and disbelief. "It tried grabbing at the chopper. Berkley lost control, and it went spinning into the camp."

Now that smell made sense.

"Crap, we need to get out of here."

"We're taking the science boat," Hatcher said. "It's the only one with sufficient fuel."

"Suits me." Kane raced over to where Taft had fallen and pulled him upright. "Wake up, Sleeping Beauty. We have to move."

Taft moaned, his face swelling from the hit he took.

"Did I win?"

"Totally," Kane quipped, guiding the mercenary to the southeast docks. "He never saw you coming."

CHAPTER 11

The *Kingsford* was in full throttle going eastbound for Coral Basin. On its decks, fourteen occupants watched the water with dreaded anticipation, fearing that hellish shape could emerge at any moment.

Never in his life did Kane ever feel unsafe on a boat of any kind. If there was something to be feared, it usually came from above in the form of a drone or helicopter. Today, it was under the sea.

Rook Island faded away into the distance, the column of smoke reaching into the heavens like ash from a volcanic eruption.

Standing near the commander were Jon and Tracie Otrin, the latter more concerned about the scar on her son's face than anything else.

"I'm alright, ma," he said.

"You sure you didn't get burned in the fire?"

Jon laughed. "If I did, the first thing to go would be my hair." He ran his hand over the shaggy fluff up there. "Still there."

Tracie smiled. "Still needs cutting." She put a finger to his widow's peak. "About an inch long and combed to the side is your best look."

"Not sure where you get your tastes, but whatever floats your boat," he said. He looked over at Kane. "So, what's your guys' story?"

The commander kept a watchful eye on the sea, waiting for a swarm of tentacles to emerge at any moment.

"We were hired by a small island nation in the area called Malau to flush out the pirate camp operating in the area. Turns out they moved beyond hijacking ships and stealing merchandise."

"Drugs," Tracie said.

Kane nodded. "Yep. Pirates like money. And there's plenty of it in the world of drugs, I'm afraid."

"You're a private contractor," Jon pointed out.

Usually, when Kane heard someone make that statement, it was with a tone of disdain. *"Oh, you're mercenary. All you care about is money."* As if anyone else on Earth did not make a living one way or another. Kane was selective in the way he picked his missions. Simply put; killing bad guys, especially when they were shooting at him, was no problem. But he was not an assassin. He had lost enough of his own people to appreciate the sanctity of life. Once, he was offered a job in which the objective was to sabotage a rival company's supply chain. By 'sabotage', they meant blow up the freight ships. To hell with the crew on board.

Not only did he tell the non-client to go to hell, but the shipping company received an anonymous tip, warning them of potential danger.

"That's right," he answered Jon.

The young man was not judgmental. On the contrary, he took a sharp interest.

"What were you before? Army? Navy?"

Kane took his eyes off the water and looked at his new friend. Tracie seemed interested too, not so much in his career, but in the way her son was energetic. He suspected she had not seen him so alive in months, if not years.

"Marines," he answered. "Eight years."

"That's awesome."

"Thinking of signing up?"

Jon's expression sank. "If I did, I'd go Army. But, I have other obligations." He enlivened once more, having thought of a new question. "You did the Crucible?"

"Hmm? Oh, yeah. Final part of boot camp."

"I've read about that while researching all the branches," Jon said. "Like I said, I'd probably go Army, because that's what my dad was. But my grandpa was in the Marines, so sometimes I think about that. Anyway, I remember him mentioning the Crucible."

It was a nostalgic memory for Kane.

"Be ready for sore feet. You'll be marching for forty-five miles in full-gear with forty-five extra pounds if you're lucky. Don't expect to get any real sleep during that time. Or food. And there's more than just marching; there's obstacle courses and simulated combat scenarios, all of which they grade you on. You see, it's meant to train you both mentally and physically. You can't always be expected to be all rested, fresh out of bed, with coffee and eggs in your belly, when shit hits the fan. Sometimes, that shit is coming at you all day and all night, and that's when you face a *real* test of character—when you keep fighting and pushing forward, even though you've been through absolute hell."

Jon remained quiet, letting the commander's words sink in. At the end of his moment, he replied with, "You and my dad would've gotten along very well. You'd've traded jabs, with him being Army and you being Marines."

Kane smiled, though also reading between the lines of what Jon said. The choice of words was specific, meaning his dad was deceased.

"There is a very good chance of that," Kane replied.

Their moment was interrupted by the *Kingsford's* first mate, who called from the observation deck.

"Hey! Any sign of it?"

"Nope," Hatcher replied.

"How fast can those things go?" Oliver asked, his gaze shifting to Tracie.

She put her hands out. "Known specimens are believed to reach speeds of twenty-five miles per hour. But that big one? Hopped up on heroin? Your guess is as good as mine."

Kane watched the water behind them. If the creature was on their tail, he was managing to keep stealthy.

"What do we do once we get to the island?" Tracie asked.

"We'll anchor in shallow water and use a raft to go ashore," he answered. "Taft has our SAT phone. We'll order ourselves a new ride from Malau. A chopper, preferably."

"Only this time, it'll be able to set down farther inland," Agent Ravee said.

"Suits me," Jon said.

"On that note," Oliver announced like the host of a game show. "We're in the final stretch!"

He proudly pointed forward.

Kane and Jon leaned over the side for a good look at their destination. Coral Basin was coming into view, its west beach appealing to the eye.

"Damn," Jon said. "If it weren't for murderous pirates and monster squids, I'd give thought to coming back to this place with a nice lounge chair."

"Ha! Can't say I blame you," Kane replied. "I, for one, could go for a tiki bar with a nice umbrella and a…"

His voice trailed off.

Jon looked at the commander, his smile vanishing after noting the hardening gaze. He turned his eyes past the bow and saw the huge red blob of mass coming straight for the bow of the *Kingsford.*

BAM!

The bow pitched, the stern threatening to dip into the waves. Everyone stumbled backward, some of them rolling across the deck in a reverse summersault.

"Shit!" Hatcher grumbled, tensing as the boat leveled out. "It's here!"

"How the hell did it get ahead of us?" Oliver shouted.

"Hopped up on drugs," Taft replied.

A second impact rocked the boat, throwing everyone aboard off balance.

"We're under attack!" Daow Aree shouted. He stood near the transom with Rudy and Eiji, hands tied behind his back. "You must unbind us so we can have a chance."

"Yeah, that's not happening," Axel said.

Kane's eyes went from the water to the wheelhouse, then back. They were not moving.

"What's happening up there?"

A sweaty, out-of-breath Ernie Cardellini stumbled out of the wheelhouse. "It stalled the engine when it hit."

There was a groan of metal followed by a heavy tilt to port.

Hearing a scraping sound on deck, Kane looked over his shoulder. The submersible was sliding out of place, coming straight at him and Jon. He grabbed the aspiring warfighter and pulled him out of the way.

BAM!

The sub hit the gunnel with enough force to bend it an inch outward.

A salty mist rose as huge red limbs ascended over the port side. Their suction cups pulsed, extending their brown claws.

Without his H&K, lost during the fight with Goro, and his secondary weapon aboard the *Grand Voyager,* Kane felt naked and vulnerable.

He held his hand out to Jon, touching the AK-47 he still kept strapped over his shoulder.

"Mind if I borrow your souvenir?"

Jon gladly handed it over. "Go nuts."

Kane did exactly that. Aiming the gun high, he fired off several bursts of ammunition. Little holes popped in the red flesh, spewing light-blue fluid.

Ravee and the other teammates joined in, pelting the swarm with lead.

The tentacles writhed like caterpillars reaching for a leaf, dripping ammonia, and spreading apart to retaliate.

One of them stretched across the deck and looped around the other side. Another slithered over the submersible, its tip moving straight for Jon.

Kane put himself between it and the teenager, thrusting the rifle muzzle point-blank into the limb. A single shot split its tip wide open, giving the tentacle the appearance of a pair of open pliers, dripping blood from their opening.

The injured tentacle retracted into the water.

Its master spewed a massive cloud of ink, darkening the blue sea around the *Kingsford.*

"It's pissed off!" Woodley shouted.

"Yeah?" Hatcher reloaded his gun. "So am I." He continued blasting into the water.

In the blink of an eye, the tentacles released the boat and vanished under the dark cloud of ink.

The men ceased fire, feeling the water shifting their boat while the huge mass below changed location.

"I don't see it," Vladik said.

"Nor I," Taft added. "You think it's gone?"

Kane shook his head. "Not hardly. Hatcher? Try again with the Shooting Star. See if you can get a lock on it."

The mercenary handed over his submachine gun and switched to the gift from his boss' mentor. He pointed it toward the sea and attempted to get a heat-signature scan.

"Nothing."

"We can still laser it," Taft said.

"We need a visual first," Hatcher replied.

As though in direct response, the huge arms rose over the stern, splashing the three prisoners with seawater.

Daow jumped away from the transom, leaving his two associates dumbfounded.

Eiji and Rudy were both caught by the shock of their sudden appearance, the latter tripping over his own feet when the water hit his eyes.

One of the tentacles, as though it had a vision of its own, came right at him.

Rudy screamed and convulsed with agony, feeling his bones crushing against one another and squishing his soft insides as he was lifted off the deck. The tentacle disappeared under the water with its prize. A moment later, a burst of blood and shredded clothes bubbled in the middle of the ink cloud.

Eiji turned forward and attempted to make a run for it. Another arm bent over the transom and came after him like a snake coming up on a mouse, only much faster.

With a striking motion, it curved its huge tip over his shoulder, the suction cup at its end snagging him with its claw.

Screaming, Eiji stumbled backward. Another tentacle emerged and grabbed ahold of his feet.

At once the two arms lifted him high into the air. As though functioning with minds of their own, they 'fought' over the victim, both pulling outward.

Eiji's body stretched like a rubber band, his spine and tendons eventually snapping, his meat splitting at the abdomen.

A bellyful of guts spilled as the two halves separated. As quickly as they appeared, the tentacles vanished.

“Damn it! I still can’t get a lock,” Hatcher said. “The thing’s too cold. The computer can’t tell it apart from the water.”

“But those missiles can hit underwater targets, right?” Tracie asked.

“As long as it’s not too deep, yeah,” he answered.

She put her hand on the submersible. “You think you can lock on to this?”

Jon approached his mother and grabbed her arm. “Wait, you’re not thinking of going down there, are you? You’ll get killed, if not by the squid, by the blast.”

She put her hand on his face. “I can set it for autopilot and have it go away from the ship. They can’t blow up the squid while it’s right next to us anyway.”

“She’s right,” Kane said. “Don’t worry, Jon. We’ll make sure she stays in one piece.” He looked at Tracie. “You’re sure you can rig the thing for autopilot?”

“Yeah, we just need to get it into the water. It won’t operate otherwise. Once I have it set, I’ll come through the top hatch and you can hoist me up with the cable.”

“Then let’s do it.”

With the help of Hatcher and Taft, he hooked the cable to the submersible.

The water swirled, alerting them to the movements of their enormous adversary. It was under the boat, prepping for another attack.

“I don’t know, man,” Jon said. “It might snatch her up before you can get the sub in the water.”

Kane thought about it for a moment, realizing he had a point.

"We need to drive it away long enough for us to set the trap." He looked across the deck in hopes of finding a fuel drum. There were none, forcing him to come up with an alternative.

"What about soundwaves?" Taft suggested, sporting one of his grenades.

All eyes went to Tracie.

"It's possible. Sound travels faster and further underwater than air. Even if the grenades don't hit it, the decibel level might be too much for it to handle."

"Works for me," Jon said.

He and Taft moved to the gunnel, each holding two grenades.

After counting down from three, they chucked them into the water.

Five seconds later, four simultaneous blasts ripped holes in the ocean's surface, which were immediately closed up.

There was another tremor of motion, followed by the scraping of the beast passing under the keel.

"There!" Axel said, pointing out to starboard. "I saw it."

"Let's go!" Kane said.

Tracie climbed aboard the submersible and gave a thumbs-up.

Taft operated the crane, lifting her six feet off the deck and gently swinging her over the side.

"Might wanna hurry," Axel called. "I think it's coming back."

Kane looked to the south. There was a splash of water and a red glimmer heading in their direction.

Taft lowered the sub until it was on the water's surface.

Tracie disappeared inside. The exterior lights came alive and its engine hummed. There was the sound of its rudders shifting and the throttle activating.

She reappeared through the hatch.

"Better move!" Axel warned. "It's coming in hot."

Tracie disconnected the cable and hung to the clamp with gloved hands. The crane lifted her from the water. Meanwhile, the submersible moved north, away from the *Kingsford*.

An impact on the starboard side shook the vessel. Arms lifted over the starboard side, ready to resume the fight.

"Don't shoot!" Kane said. It was an order intended for himself as much as the others, as his instinct to blast those disgusting tentacles had his face beet red.

They hovered over the deck, dripping their rancid secretions.

Jon hugged his mother as she was set down, anticipating a horrible result should the plan fail.

All at once, the arms returned to the water. A concentrated stream surged in a straight line, the squid's siphon pushing it under the boat towards the source of the soundwaves.

Everyone looked out to port.

The yellow-white titanium hull was quickly enveloped in red. The creature's mantle breached the surface, its fins waving from its bullet-shaped body. For a split second, its white beak was visible, as was its huge tongue.

It pulled the sub close, crunching one of its ballasts with a powerful bite.

"Do it, Hatcher," Kane ordered.

"You got it."

Hatcher pointed the Shooting Star and put the target front and center in its targeting system. The computer detected the submersible and locked on to it, flashing red to inform its operator that it was ready to fire.

He let it fly.

The missile zoomed from its launcher directly to its target. In under a second, it made impact.

BOOM!

An eruption of metal, water, and flesh reached high into the air.

The team leaned away, feeling a gust of air carrying heat, smoke, and a putrid odor.

Pieces of tentacles started raining down as though they were in a storm from hell. Ink and blood expanded in all directions in a vast cloud.

In the middle of it all, the ravaged corpse of the giant squid, torn wide open, its head turned to minced meat, floated over the waves.

The beast was dead.

"Bullseye," Hatcher exclaimed.

Ernie and Oliver pumped their fists on the observation deck, cheering the victory.

"Yes!" Jon shouted. He hugged his mom. "Good thinking on using the sub."

She chuckled. "Hopefully the Institute won't be too pissed that I let it get blown up."

Kane smiled and watched the corpse drifting in the gradually calming water. "If that's the worst of our problems, I'll take it."

CHAPTER 12

The two fishermen were moving all over the boat, bringing tools, oil jugs, and spare parts to the *Kingsford's* engine.

"Bear with us, lady and gentlemen," Ernie said. "The squid did a number on us. We'll be out of here before you know it."

"No worries," Kane said.

Those on deck were preoccupied with a new spectacle taking place before them. In the minutes following the squid's explosive demise, the sea abruptly began to churn around its body. One by one, the natural inhabitants of the sea followed the scent of blood to the corpse and began feasting on the free meal. After fifteen minutes, it was a full-on feeding frenzy.

Dorsal fins cleaved the water as various species of sharks helped themselves to the buffet.

"Is it too late for a clever one-liner?" Hatcher said. "For lunch, I'm thinking calamari!" Kane closed his eyes. "Yes. It is too late."

"Eh. What fun are you?"

Taft had moved up onto the flying deck, watching the island of Coral Basin through the window of the bridge. It was so close; less than a quarter mile away, its tropical interior looking more welcoming with every passing moment.

"Geez. At this point, I'm thinking we could just paddle our way over there."

"Don't tempt me," Vladik said. He stood guard next to Daow, who had remained silent since the death of the squid. During the attack, behind his fear, there was a hint of giddiness, for he believed the monster from the deep held the key to his escape. The odds may have been against him, but it was better than being shipped off for trial and imprisonment.

Ravee, sensing the pirate's sense of defeat, could not help himself. He stepped in front of Daow and leaned close to his face.

"That's right. Sulk."

Daow's glare tightened, his eye appearing almost redder, as though his veins were bleeding into it.

The agent stepped away, hoping his prisoner was unaware his attempt to intimidate was successful.

He joined Kane, Jon, and Tracie on the portside, watching the feeding frenzy.

"It's amazing, how destructive some things may be," he said. "That's a creature born of nature, and it almost had us at its mercy, even though we had weapons and technology on our side."

"It truly is," Tracie replied. Whilst Ravee's tone was of fascination, hers was a little more somber. "The squid had probably never exited the trench before in its life. Someone of such immense size, in an area where people fish and a company was building a rig, would've been hard not to be spotted at least once. It may be a predator, but it was not a monster. Not until recently. In its mind, all it was doing was scavenging. Not even killing. Next thing it knew, it ingested a man-made substance that corrupted its brain and drove it into a frenzy. Had it not been for that, none of us would know it existed.

Even down in the trench, it probably would have avoided us."

She sighed.

"Such a remarkable creature, destroyed, not by missiles, but by hubris and greed."

She could hear Daow sticking his tongue out. For a sinister pirate, he seemed to enjoy acting like a four-year-old.

"Whoa!" Taft pointed at the frenzy. "Looks like a few of our buddies don't like the sushi."

As he spoke, three of the sharks broke away from the squid and started swimming southeast.

"Hmm." Tracie took notice of the haste in their movements. "They're moving awfully fast."

"Maybe it's too chewy," Hatcher joked.

His laugh was cut short by the sight of another shark fleeing the area. Then another, and another, and another, all heading southeast at high speed.

All at once, the remainder of the group departed in one direction.

Kane followed them with his eyes until they disappeared under the water.

"This isn't my area of expertise, but I have a feeling that's not normal."

"It isn't," Tracie said. "There's only one reason such a large school would flee from an area with easily accessible sustenance."

Taft swallowed. "And that is?"

"If they detect a larger, deadlier predator in the area."

Kane inhaled. The sharks had fled southeast, indicating whatever scared them off was coming from the northwest.

"Fuck…"

It passed through the waves like a torpedo, under its brethren, breaching the water near the *Kingsford* port quarter.

With an explosion of seawater, the squid unfolded its many arms like an umbrella from hell. A giant white beak parted, its tongue unraveling, ready to shred the meat off the bones of anything unlucky enough to be placed there.

Huge arms, many of them dark and scaly in texture after roasting in burning fuel, lashed at the deck. The two longest tentacles punched their clubbed ends through the hull of the ship, tearing through the staterooms, galley, and processing area.

The *Kingsford* tipped backward, its bow raising ten degrees.

Ernie and Oliver arrived topside, the former shouting, "What's going on?"

The answer literally grabbed ahold of him. The captain wailed in his husky voice, getting increasingly chaotic as he approached the beak.

Keeping its mouth visible for everyone to watch, the squid clamped its beak over the fisherman's body. The tongue passed over him, literally ripping his clothes and flesh in long, smooth movements.

More arms pummeled the ship, striking with enough impact to lacerate the hull.

"Jesus, how strong is this thing?" Taft called out.

The boat shook under their feet.

Kane struck the creature near the mouth with rifle fire, driving it below the surface.

Its arms continued the punishment, the two clubbed tentacles now forming a twine over the wheelhouse and its flying deck. Taft leapt for dear life, the structure imploding directly behind him.

Pieces rained down on the main deck, skidding in all directions while the beast continued rocking the boat.

Oliver was moving to the center of the deck, dragging a large, cube-shaped object.

"There's no way around it," he said. "We're going down. This may not last us long against the squid, but it beats…"

A swipe of an arm connected with his face, taking his head right off the neck. Oliver's body collapsed, the red stump gushing blood.

Tracie yelped, unable to take her eyes off the headless corpse.

"Keep hitting it," Kane ordered his team. "Tracie… TRACIE!" She looked at him. "Inflate that raft. Get it ready."

She snapped out of it and walked around the large yellow cube in search of the ripcord.

The mercenaries sprayed bullets into the water and the sky, failing to repel the small army of muscular arms.

One of them struck the deck, launching bolts from their place.

Vladik ejected his magazine and grabbed for a fresh one.

"Look out!" Hatcher called to him.

Vladik looked straight ahead. Right in front of him was a huge tentacle moving horizontally, its first five feet of length stiff and rigid.

"BLECH!"

It punched through his chest and lifted him up like a fish on a spear.

"Vladik!" Axel shouted. He hit the tentacle with a few rounds, the beast seeming to hardly notice as it brought the dead mercenary under the frothing water. He moved to the transom, spraying the remainder of his magazine into the mass below. "Die, devil!"

SPLASH!

When the mist cleared, the team of mercenaries watched in horror while Axel was lifted ten feet high, his waist compressed by one of the arms. It waved him back and forth like a toy plane, before deliberately crashing him headfirst into the hull of the ship.

POP!

Blood and guts burst from the point of impact.

Hatcher tossed a grenade. It hit the water and detonated, kicking up mist. The beast was undeterred, too entrenched in the slaughter of the *Kingsford* and everyone on it.

Taft tossed a grenade. Same result.

"Damn it, the thing's not going away," he said.

"It's looking for its next fix," Kane replied.

"Yeah?" Hatcher said. "Too bad we can't just direct it to the yachts we left behind—" A tentacle emerged behind him, catching him on the small of his back. Hatcher yelled out, eyes wide, the nerve pain instantaneous.

Kane reached out and caught him before he could faceplant. Gently, he lowered the soldier onto the deck.

"AH!" Hatcher exclaimed, arms tense.

"How bad is it?" Kane asked. "Can you move your legs?"

"N-no!"

Another tentacle swung over their heads with lightning force. Woodley turned around after shooting into the water, just in time to see the rubbery limb coming at him.

It struck across his center, sending him flying far into the ocean. His arms flapped in midair, as did his intestines as his lower half separated from the rest of him.

"Good God!" Taft exclaimed.

The boat shuddered once more. They heard the groaning of metal and the rushing of water.

"There's no stopping it," Tracie said. "It's not gonna quit until it's dead or gets drugs in its system!"

Jon was kneeling beside her, stricken with fear, watching the sanctuary that was Coral Basin. It was so close, but may as well have been on the other side of the galaxy.

All they needed was fifteen or twenty good minutes, and they could easily paddle to shore.

The bow began tilting upward, the stern compartments flooding. Pieces of the crushed wheelhouse broke away and rolled all the way to the transom, joining all sorts of other unsecured items, including weapons from deceased mercenaries, and Tracie's necropsy supplies.

Jon rose to his knees.

In that pile was one of the two-ounce syringes he had brought to his mother.

"It needs a fix," he muttered.

He rose to his feet and sprinted for the transom.

"Jon!" Tracie called after him.

He arrived at the pile of wreckage, grabbed the syringe, and for good measure, picked up the late Woodley's H&K. Slinging it over his shoulder, he ran up the slope of the *Kingsford's* deck and rejoined the others.

"You!" he shouted at Daow. He knelt by the pirate and begin frisking him.

"And here I thought *I* was the pickpocket," the pirate scumbag quipped.

Jon shoved his hand into Daow's left side pocket and pulled out the baggie of heroin he had shown off during their first interaction.

"Anyone have water?"

Taft handed him a canteen. "Are you doing what I think you're doing?"

"Yeah I am," Jon said.

"How the hell are you gonna get that needle into that thing?" Tracie asked. "I mean, it should be enough to penetrate the skin, but there's no way to get close enough to the beast without getting torn apart."

"Trust me, Mom!" he said.

Tracie went quiet. Her motherly tendency welled up a monologue of how she did not want him to risk himself. But he was his father's son, strong-willed, and courageous.

It was a dirty feeling, prepping a dose of heroin for injection. If it weren't for movies, he would have no clue what he was doing.

He stood up and held the syringe like a dagger, needle pointed down, its body filled with two ounces of brown liquid.

"Get in the raft," he said.

"Wait, kid!" Kane said. "I should be the one…"

"I need you to get my mom to that island!" Jon shouted.

"Kid!"

The boat shook, throwing Kane off balance. The final plunge began, the ocean swallowing the stern and gradually slurping up the rest of the boat.

Waiting under the waves was the beast, watching with demented eyes.

Jon took a breath and whispered to his dad's spirit for any help he'd be willing to give.

Having done that, he went into action.

Jon sprang off the boat into the water, syringe raised over his shoulder. He passed through a mess of tentacles, into the ocean, where he sank onto the squid's mantle.

Rubbery flesh inflated underneath his body like a partially inflated balloon in need of more air. Gritting his teeth, he put the needle to the skin and pressed down. The needle bent, threatening to snap against the thick flesh.

Come on! Come on!

Gradually, the tip began to penetrate. The needle straightened, slowly sinking into the creature's body.

Jon pushed on the plunger, injecting the creature with the mixture.

In the span of a heartbeat, the tentacles stiffened. The beast drifted away from the boat, no longer interested in wreaking havoc. Before, it had ingested the substance orally, but this was a pure injection straight into the bloodstream.

A high it never knew existed flooded its brain.

Feeling a rush, the beast jetted water through its siphon.

Jon felt a rush as if he was on an underwater rollercoaster. His world went dark, the current blinding him, his hand clasped over the syringe.

He tried to scream, but couldn't. His vision went blank—as blank as death. There was no pain, no fear. Just emptiness.

"No! NOOO!" Tracie slammed her fist against the gunnel.

"I don't see him," Ravee shouted.

"Nor do I," Taft replied.

The *Kingsford* was almost halfway down now, the water reaching the raft and survivors.

Kane put his hands on Tracie's shoulders.

"We have to go!"

"No, I'm not leaving him!" she shouted.

Kane gave another look to the sea. The squid was gone and had taken her son with it.

He hated being in this position. One did not need to be a parent to understand the anguish Tracie was going through right now. But the creature would inevitably be back. Given its anatomy, there was no telling how long the fix would last it. It was a monster with a body length of nearly fifty feet, and that did not even account for its many huge arms. Two ounces, while fatal to any human, was probably barely a snort for that thing.

"I'm sorry, Tracie, but we have to go. Or it will come back."

With tears streaming down her face, Tracie lowered herself into the raft. Kane and Taft lifted Hatcher up and got him aboard, then got themselves in. Ravee sat in the back with Daow, who stared across the small boat at his former prisoner.

She burned him with vengeful eyes.

"This is all your fault."

Daow had no remorse. “I can say I’m sorry he’s gone. I actually kinda liked him. Probably would’ve been fun to have him on my team.”

Tracie’s hand inched to the side, on the verge of going for Taft’s firearm. In the end, she managed to hold back.

The *Kingsford* rolled to starboard, its bow slipping under the sea. Riding a large wave, the group began paddling to shore, not one of them daring to utter a word about what had just happened.

CHAPTER 13

It took twenty-six minutes for them to paddle their way to the shore of Coral Basin. In the span of the small journey, nobody spoke a word. At most, Taft, Kane, and Ravee gave a comforting shoulder tap to the numb Dr. Tracie Otrin. She was glazy-eyed, possibly in shock, unable to do anything except rest against the hull of the raft.

Hatcher maintained a strained face the entire time, the hit of morphine administered by Taft doing little against his agonizing pain. He still could not move his legs, strongly indicating major spinal injury.

The raft touched the sandbar on the island's west shore. Taft and Kane stepped out and pulled it onto dry land. The land in front of them was wide open and fairly level, with some boulders and trees thirty yards straight ahead, and some green hills and trees to their right.

Taft put his hands on his knees, completely spent. "Thank God." Immediately, he felt embarrassed, mouthing *sorry* to Tracie in fear of coming off as insensitive.

She shook her head. "No, no. It's okay." She looked to the sea. "It's perfectly alright. As far as I'm concerned, it's your duty to live. I don't just mean survive to see another day. I mean truly live your lives. That's what Jon would want. That's what his father wanted for us." She cleared her throat and wiped her eyes. "I'm gonna refuse to cry anymore. I'm not saying I'll succeed—I probably won't. But I'll give it my best shot."

"He's a good kid," Kane said. He took a seat on the beach next to her while Taft tended to Hatcher and Ravee moved Daow farther inland. The agent kept an eye on the conversation, taking to heart what the grieving mother was saying.

"He is," Tracie said with a smile. For some reason, neither of them felt it appropriate to use the term 'was'. It felt inappropriate, and somehow *inaccurate.* Neither spoke of the thought, figuring they were subconsciously thinking of him being alive in spirit.

"He took a liking to you," Tracie continued.

"Well…" Kane shrugged, playing it cool. "I *did* save you guys from the pirates."

"Technically it was me who sniped the guys who were gonna put him over the fire!" Hatcher shouted in a strained voice.

Kane and even Tracie chuckled at that. Even with a broken back, the guy made sure not to lose his wit.

"You all were great," Tracie said. She wiped another tear. "Damn, I'm sorry."

"Oh, don't be ridiculous," Kane said. "Don't even think of apologizing. As John Wayne once said in *She Wore a Yellow Ribbon,* 'Don't apologize. It shows weakness.'"

Tracie laughed gently. "Oh, great. Another fan of the Duke."

"You have a problem with the Duke?"

"Only the fact that my late husband and Jon have always been obsessed with him," she replied. "No wonder the man upstairs sent you as our guardian angel."

Kane treasured that remark.

"On the contrary, I consider your boy my guardian angel. He was fast on his feet and quick to come up with ideas. If not for him, we'd all be lost at sea right now."

Tracie nodded. "On that note, I just remembered… damn! You lost a few guys out there too."

Kane watched the water, the final resting place for his teammates. "They were fighters. Trust me, we mourn with cigars and whiskey. While we strive to live to see the end of each mission, we all agree there's no better way to conclude our time on earth than in a good, meaningful fight."

"My husband felt the same way," Tracie said. She looked at the mercenary commander. "What were their names?"

"Woodley, Axel, and Vladik," he replied. "Good guys. In spite of what people may think of mercenaries, they weren't mindless killers. They were good-hearted men who went out on their own terms. Maybe they weren't anticipating being bested by a giant squid of all things, but they went out fighting."

Ravee took a seat on a rock twenty yards inland. "Do we have an ETA on pickup?"

"About two hours," Taft replied. "Until then, there's really nothing we can do except wait."

And wait they did, watching the surf roll up on shore. It was a comforting silence which allowed Kane and Tracie to reflect on their lives and the sacrifices made by others.

Like all things, the peace came to an end. In this case, it was from Agent Ravee calling to Kane.

"You might want to come take a look at this!"

Kane and Tracie stood up and ran near the boulders where Ravee and Daow were waiting.

On the other side of the boulder was a shallow pit, approximately a meter in diameter, and filled with the charred remains of tinder.

"A campfire," Kane said.

Tracie pointed twenty degrees to the left. "There's another one."

Kane inspected the coals inside each of them, his face rapidly getting tense. "These aren't old. This one's still warm."

"Do people usually camp out on this island?" Tracie asked.

"They might anchor offshore and overnight in their boats. At most, they'll maybe come ashore and explore a bit," Ravee explained. "But this looks like someone had a settlement here."

"I agree with that," Kane said. "You can see where one of the guys was sleeping." He ran his foot over the dirt, uprooting some grass, and revealing a small, brass item.

"Is that what I think it is?" Tracie asked.

Kane picked it up and held it in the light. "A bullet cartridge. Nine-millimeter." He looked at Daow, ready to ask if he had people on this island.

Interestingly, the look on Daow's face was an answer in itself. Had he had a secret group on Coral Basin, he would be grinning ear-to-ear, anticipating a grand assault. Interestingly enough, he looked angry, that ugly eye of his burning into the empty cartridge.

Somebody was here on this island, and it was someone he did not like.

BANG!

Ravee yelled out and reeled backward, his left shoulder spilling blood. He hit the ground near Tracie, who backed away, startled by the sudden change in events.

More gunshots rang out, the bullets deliberately landing near her feet.

Everyone froze, having received the message loud and clear. For good measure, the leader of the unseen attackers spelled it out in plain, fluent English.

"Anyone moves, the lady is the first to die!"

Kane bitterly raised his hands. Part of the profession was knowing when he was bested.

Sons of bitches! Of all people to lose to, it's a band of ratty pirates!

Twelve men emerged from hiding, some armed with nine-millimeter pistols, others holding Russian AK-74s.

Like ranchers herding cattle, they corralled the team back at the beach, securing any weapons they could find.

Taft was last to be disarmed. He stood in a brief standoff with the pirates, his pride getting in the way of him relinquishing his weapon. Only the fact that innocents were at gunpoint made him swallow that pride and hand over the guns.

Ravee stood on the shore with Kane, while pressing a rag to his bullet wound. The pirates fanned out, keeping them in the path of an inescapable firing line. Their clothing was long, oversized, and full of tears.

The only exception was their leader. He was a head taller than the others, was a tad more well-kept in his appearance, sporting a patchy beard and long black hair. His clothes were a better fit, his grey shirt tucked into some tactical pants.

He swept over the group with a murderous gaze, cracking a smile when he settled on Daow Aree.

"I've been waiting to find you for a long time. But my, oh my, did I not expect this."

Taft leaned over to Agent Ravee. "You know this guy?"

Ravee nodded, his expression nearly as bitter as Daow's. "Chao Fah. Daow's rival."

True to his personality, Taft sniggered. "Daow and Chao. You guys have the same mother by any chance?"

A tilt of Chao's head informed one of the pirate subordinates to make an example of him. Taft was struck in the face and knocked down.

"No, not the same mother," Chao said. "Mine was no whore."

Daow spat at him and cursed in his native language.

Chao laughed, taking immense pleasure in his adversary's rage. He gave a long inquisitive look at the men in black standing in front of him, taking particular interest in Hatcher.

"Looks like you have seen better days. Shipwreck?"

"You could say that," Kane said. His gut warned him that this group was unaware of the giant squid.

"And you were here to hunt him," Chao said. "Normally, I'd thank you. This is actually the greatest gift anyone's ever brought me. You gave me Daow, the son of a whore who thought he could be king! Without even firing a shot, I did not have to bring him down. Where is Goro? Eiji? Ban-Jen? The rest of his clan?"

"Having a cookout," Ravee said.

"Ah! Hell. You did all of that? All by yourselves?" Chao asked.

"Eh." Taft shrugged. "You could say we had a little help."

Chao was not sure what to make of that. Nor did he care.

"You are an agent of Malau," he said. "You hired these people to bring Daow down."

"'Bring Daow down'…Say that five times fast," Taft muttered.

He was struck again by one of the pirates.

"I suppose I should thank you," Chao continued, his attention now on Kane. "But, you see, we have a little problem. See, we have three cruisers that have gone missing inexplicably around this island. Now that you're here, I think I have my answer. Maybe it was a mistake in identity; you probably thought they were Daow's men. But all the same, I can't let that slide."

"It wasn't them," Tracie said.

"Oh!" Chao exclaimed. "You sound awfully sure, woman. Please explain to me, if it wasn't your people who killed our patrols, who was it."

Tracie went silent, knowing the type of reaction the answer would get.

Taft, however, could not help himself.

"Would you believe us if we said it was a giant squid?"

Chao snorted. "Oh, is that right? Let me guess, it rose from the depths, right?"

"Yes!" Taft said enthusiastically.

Chao smiled, enjoying this little back and forth with the American mercenary. "And it attacked you too! That's why you are shipwrecked."

"Yes!" Taft exclaimed.

"He catches on quick," Hatcher said.

Taft pointed a finger at Daow. "He doesn't like this son of a whore. Obviously, he can't be all *that* bad."

The group broke out in laughter, some of it genuine, some of it nervousness.

Chao reached around his back and lifted a radio. He raised it to his lips and spoke to someone else in Thai.

Ravee laughed. "What? You actually going to see if there's a squid out there? That why you're telling your remaining boaters to move to the west?"

Chao clipped his radio back to his waist. "As fascinating as that idea is, I'm more interested in making sure you don't have any other personnel out there. Don't worry, if there are, we'll take care of them."

Kane chose not to say anything. If they wanted to find out what truly sunk their boats, they may as well find out for themselves… up close and personal.

"First, let me deal with my old friend." Chao stepped in front of Daow, signaling to one of his men to knock the disgraced adversary to his knees. The red-eyed pirate hit the sand, baring teeth, refusing to look his new captor in the eye.

"How pathetic," Chao continued. "You really thought you were better than me. You said I was nothing, and bragged how you would have control over all of Southeast Asia, as though you were gonna take over the world."

Daow snarled at him. "You are nothing more than a puppy, nipping at the heels of larger dogs. You're waste. You're a scrap. You can barely get more than twenty followers. Nobody likes you! Nobody has confidence in your leadership. You are nobody and will always be nobody."

Chao sniggered and pulled his pistol from his belt. "At least my mother didn't leave me behind a dumpster while she was riding cowboy."

He put the pistol to Daow's forehead.

The pirate cringed.

This was worse than any fate he could have anticipated. Rotting in prison would even have been preferable. Even becoming squid food. Anything other than dying on his knees in front of Chao Fah.

It was the second-to-last thing to go through Daow Aree's mind—the last was the bullet from Chao's gun.

He watched the dead body fall forward, pooling blood in the sand, listening to the echo of the gunshot. After allowing a moment for the tension to settle in, he turned the gun to Kane.

"What a shame," he said. "You and I would have made a beautiful team."

Kane allowed himself an ever-so-slight grin. "In your dreams."

He stared into the muzzle of the gun, anticipating the burning flash.

***

He was almost there.

Every muscle in Jon's body was screaming at him. The pain and exhaustion played tricks on his mind, making him feel as though the island was moving away from him as he swam towards it.

When he got carried away with the squid, he had blacked out. In those moments, he was sure he was dead. He had to have been. No way could anyone survive such a crazy endeavor.

Next thing he knew, he was lost in a current. His mind returned to him, his father's voice yelling at him, "Go, Jon! Get moving! Get to it!"

When he broke the surface, he was several hundred feet south of where the *Kingsford* had sunk. Through the lapping water, he failed to get a visual on his mom or Kane's team. But common sense was enough for him to surmise they were heading for the island.

The only way for him to regroup was to swim.

Jon considered himself a good swimmer, but this was a feat that would test even Olympic champions. He failed to give up, reminding himself that this was no place to die. His dad would not stand for it, his mother could not live with it.

Even as his muscles felt as though they would snap like rubber bands, he pushed forward, aiming for a little panhandle on the island's southwest corner.

Shallow water never felt so good.

His feet touched down. After a few more yards, he was able to collapse to his hands and knees and crawl to the shoreline.

There, he rolled to his back and rested.

He did it. He made it. Life was destined to cling to him a little while longer. It was a fact his body would remind him of twenty-four/seven for at least three days. In a sense, he dreaded waking up tomorrow morning. The muscle cramps and soreness would be unlike anything he had ever experienced. In the end, it was also a reminder of the perseverance his dad had instilled in him.

That being said, I think I'm gonna lay here a while.

He shut his eyes and allowed himself to rest.

BANG!

He shot up to the sound of a pistol shot. It came from the interior of the small island.

Jon rolled to his knees, grimacing as he stood up. He nearly fell after getting caught off guard by the sight of a small boat wreckage. It was a skiff. By the looks of it, it was used by the pirates who had boarded the *Kingsford*. Sticking out of its bow was a large machete.

It was all that remained of the boat, as everything else was lost to sea.

The sound of voices brought Jon's attention back to whatever was taking place north of him. He gripped the H&K 416, hoping the rounds in the magazine were still good. During his swim, he refused to let go of the weapon. While its weight wasn't helping matters, he knew he did not want to be on the island unarmed, especially if he were to end up alone.

One thing was for sure; he was not alone.

He moved inland, scaling a small green hill. Lowering himself to the cover of some tall grass, he got a visual on what was going on.

"You've got to be kidding me."

There were twelve pirates standing in front of Kane's group and his mother. Daow was dead, the leader of the new group pointing his gun at Kane. The Marine did not plead or give any signs of distress. He stood there like a man and waited for whatever outcome came his way.

Jon knew the outcome. He was a dead man… unless the odds shifted.

He swallowed. Everything hurt. His head was still spinning, his heart racing. He kept his finger off the trigger, worried that the shakes would set off an accidental discharge.

How could anyone fight like this?

It was in that moment, a new voice spoke to him. This time, it was not his father's, but Kane's.

Jon thought about the Crucible and the images he had seen on the internet demonstrating what it was like.

All this time, he focused on the wrong thing. It was not important to know what the Crucible was like, but what it was meant to teach.

"…You see, it's meant to train you both mentally and physically. You can't always be expected to be all rested, fresh out of bed, with coffee and eggs in your belly, when shit hits the fan. Sometimes, that shit is coming at you all day and all night, and that's when you face a real test of character—when you keep fighting and pushing forward, even though you've been through absolute hell."

He inhaled through his nose and gripped his weapon.

"Showtime."

Resting on his stomach, he aimed the weapon at the group of pirates, and squeezed the trigger.

BANG! BANG! BANG! BANG!

Chao jumped back, alarmed by both the unexpected sounds of gunfire and the sight of two of his pirates spiraling to the ground, having taken fatal hits.

Tracie crouched. "What the… Who's doing that?"

Kane looked to the figure in the hill and smiled. "My guardian angel."

Tracie, understanding who he was referring to, felt a chill run through her body. "Jon?"

Kane, Ravee, and Taft raced into action, throwing themselves into the flustered pirate crowd.

The commander closed in on one of the filthy scumbags, wrestling his AK-74 from his grasp and caving his face in with a devasting blow with its butt. He pivoted to his left and squeezed the trigger, blowing holes in two other pirates.

Taft was a little more selective in who he went after. For him, it was the pirate henchman who had repeatedly struck him, per Chao's orders. With a knife-hand strike, he chopped the heathen in the throat, disarmed him of his rifle, and put a round through his chest.

Ravee was a little less graceful in his movements. Limited by his injury, he tackled one of the pirates like a football player, driving him backward before headbutting him repeatedly with his helmet.

With the enemy combatant dying of a skull fracture, the agent took his pistol and joined the party.

The remaining pirates were cut down to size. When dealing with unarmed enemies, they were tough and mighty. But when those enemies turned the tide, they fell apart like dominoes.

Kane took another shot, popping the head of the second-to-last pirate, with Chao as the last man standing.

Machine gun fire from the west corrected him of that fact. Three boats cruised offshore, heading northward, the pirates on deck blasting at the mercenaries.

Hatcher, scowling in endless pain, rolled to the raft. He pulled the Shooting Star over the hull and forced himself onto his belly, taking a sniper position with the homing missile launcher.

He locked on to the rear of the boats. As soon as he saw the red flash, he let the missile fly.

BOOM!

The target came apart in a hundred different pieces, as did those on board.

Hatcher raised a fist. “Yeah!”

The other boats circled back, abandoning their leader, for they were not willing to contend with superior firepower.

Unfortunately for them, they were only heading towards a worse fate.

A mountain of water rose between the two boats, taking on a shade of red, as the gargantuan squid emerged.

Its mind fried from the recent heroin dose, it was on the warpath, craving more of the drug and willing to kill as many humans as possible to get it.

Tentacles lashed across the water, striking one of the boats across the hull. It flipped over, its three pirates skipping across the water like flat stones.

The beast turned to the other vessel, grabbing ahold of it and pulling it close. The arms interloped overtop of it like folding hands, completely covering the machine and the men aboard. Their screams intensified, their gunfire doing nothing to repel the beast as it tightened its grasp.

There was a muffled sound of "AAAAGGGHHH… BLEEEGGGHHH" as they were compressed into smudges of red flesh.

The squid moved in on the stragglers, plucking them out of the water one at a time, letting its beak and tongue have the joy of ending their lives. Surrounded by a red haze, it moved closer to the shallows in search of more victims and sources of the drug.

"Let's not wait here," Kane said. "That thing's got a hell of a reach."

Tracie and Taft put Hatcher's arms around their shoulders and pulled him inland, while Ravee towed the raft and Shooting Star.

"Where's Jon?" Tracie asked.

Kane looked at the hill. Jon wasn't there.

Pistol shots rang out from the other side, providing him with the explanation. Jon was on the run, chased by a crazed Chao Fah who wanted vengeance for having his sinister plan foiled.

He slammed a fresh mag into his AK-74 and took off over the hill.

Jon tucked his head down, hearing the whistle of a third pistol shot zip by his head. The pirate leader was yelling in his native language. Jon had no idea what was being said, but considering what just happened, it was probably very mean comments, to put it mildly.

A gust of cool air hit his face as Jon skipped over the rocky surface of the island's panhandle.

He reached the edge, ending up exactly where he came ashore.

"Crap…"

The pirate appeared behind him, huffing and puffing, face red, gun pointed.

"What? You're no soldier. You're just a kid!" He shook with anger, pointing his elbow over at the beach area where his men were killed. "Look at what you have done!"

Jon rolled his shoulders. "I know what I've done. That was my ma over there. You never know how long you're gonna have them. I wasn't gonna let you take any of our time away from us."

"Oh, how cute," the pirate said.

BANG!

His shoulder opened up, sending the pirate into a spin before he collapsed on the rocks.

Jon was relieved to see Kane running over to him. "Good timing."

"You too!" the Marine replied.

They slapped hands, ready to return to the beach.

Bursting from the shallow water came an array of serpentine arms. They stretched over the rocks, one of them knocking Kane backward with a blow to the chest.

As he hit the rocks, he heard two screams.

One was from the pirate Chao Fah, who was being pulled into the water while clawing his fingers into the rocks and soil. The other was Jon, kicking his legs in a futile effort to prevent himself from getting lassoed.

The pirate managed to wedge his fingers into the tight space between two rocks. He clung for dear life, looking at Kane, begging like the puppy Daow claimed him to be.

Frustrated and impatient, the squid brought another tentacle overtop of him and hammered it down, pinning his arms. The one around his legs pulled.

Bones snapped and flesh tore.

Still reaching with his stumps, Chao was dragged to sea, his severed arms still clinging to the rocks.

Kane, now back on his feet, laid eyes on Jon. He was belly down, much like Chao before him, grabbing ahold of whatever he could while the squid tried to pull him into the water.

Other arms came at him.

Kane ducked, keeping his head by avoiding a slash. He watched the beast's face, peering out of the water with its eyes.

He lined his iron sights with one of those eyes and squeezed the trigger. Several holes popped around the cephalopod's face, forming a semi-circular pattern, ending with the explosion of its eye.

Its arms coiled backward like ants racing to the aid of their queen. Only one remained outstretched, save for its last few feet, which had wrapped around Jon's legs.

Even in pain, it was unwilling to let him go.

Kane checked his magazine. It was empty.

"Shit."

Jon cocked his head to his right. "There!"

Kane looked to what he was addressing, spotting the skiff wreckage and the machete sticking out of it.

Talk about perfect.

He raced over there, pulled the blade free, and ran to Jon. With three hacking motions, he severed the tentacle, freeing his new friend.

Jon stood up and ran to the hill alongside the commander, narrowly avoiding the reach of those tentacles.

They linked up with the others on the main beach.

Tracie lowered Hatcher to the ground and ran to her son, embracing him with a hug so tight, it nearly matched the power of the tentacles he escaped.

"Oh, God, I thought I lost you."

"I'm still here," he said.

"What's next?" Taft asked. "We just gonna wait here and hope the thing doesn't snatch the next chopper out of the air?"

"There's plenty of room for them to set down," Ravee said. "It's possible."

"And leave that thing to ambush other unsuspecting vessels?" Hatcher said. He shook his head. "No way."

The team looked at him. Without him even saying so, they knew what he was about to suggest.

"Hatcher, we might be able to fix you up," Taft said.

"It's not about that," Hatcher said. "Well, sort of. I don't want to spend my days in a wheelchair, unable to wipe my own ass. Even if they can do some work on me, I'll never be able to do what I want." He looked Kane in the eye. "I live for the action, boss. This isn't some 'woe is me' suicidal thing. We're fighters. Let me finish my fight."

Kane looked at the Shooting Star, lying at Ravee's feet.

"Just help me get in the raft," Hatcher added. "Lock on to my heat signature, send that squid bye-bye."

Kane digested the request, and answered by putting his heels together and giving the soldier a salute. It was the first time since the service he had made such a gesture.

"If you insist…" Taft lowered his buddy onto the raft, positioning him so he could paddle himself out.

"Taft… one thing," Hatcher said.

"Yeah?"

"Get a girlfriend, why don't ya?"

Taft chuckled. "Just because you say so, I will."

He and Kane pushed the raft over the beach and into the water. They went out until they were knee-deep, Hatcher taking over from there.

Straining, he ran the paddle through the water, taking the yellow inflatable farther out.

"Come on, squiddy-squid-squid!" he called out. "Looking for a buzz? I got something here that'll hit hard and fast! Come get it!"

Kane picked up the Shooting Star, put his eye to the targeting screen, and zoomed in on Hatcher's heat signature.

The red light flashed, the weapon ready to fire.

"Ah-ha! Is that you?" Hatcher shouted.

A mountain of water rolled in front of him. It split apart, unveiling the colossal drug-addicted beast. Arms uncoiled from its center, exposing its beak and one remaining eye.

"Let's do it! Let's get high!"

He threw his hands up and accepted his fate.

The beast seized Hatcher and pulled him to its mouth, unaware of the explosive projectile closing in from the beach.

BOOM!

The blast was one of pure gore, the squid having taken the hit directly. Its head was gone, its arms and guts spewing in a red and blue tidal wave. Its mantle rolled with the surf, gradually deflating as everything poured out into the open sea.

Kane dropped the Shooting Star. Its last rocket was spent, having been put to good use.

He refused to be sad. As he had explained to Tracie about the others, he would have a cigar and some whiskey in Hatcher's honor. He went out like a warrior should, not just in battle, but saving his friends.

He took a seat on the beach, confident that no other killer squids were out to ruin his day.

Jon sat next to him, exhaling sharply, his muscles reminding him of their soreness.

"Well, Mom, this was quite the trip," he said. "Looking forward to making your report to the Institute?"

She chuckled and joined them in rest. "It's gonna be unique, that's for sure."

They rested in the peace of the early afternoon sun, appreciating each other's company.

"With the pirates gone, the inflow of drugs in Malau will be halted," Ravee said proudly. "But we'll stay vigilant. You never know when trouble should arise again."

"If it does, you'll be there to handle it," Taft said.

Ravee nodded. It was not just a compliment, but a calling. He had a new appreciation for the gift of life and the quality of how it was lived.

Jon ran his hand over his hair. He pulled his dad's bandanna out of his pants pocket and went to put it on, struggling to fit it over his hair.

"Okay, Mom. You'll get your wish. When we get home, I'm getting this hair cut. What was it you said you like? An inch long up top?"

Tracie ran her hand over his hair. "Mm. I think it might need to be a little shorter."

"A buzzcut?"

She smiled with the purest of joy. "Shaved."

Jon froze, his heart flooding with emotion from the meaning of her response.

"You're sure you'll be okay with it?"

She nodded, her arm around his shoulders. "It's your calling. I think you need to answer it. If Army service is what you are meant for, then that's what you should do."

Jon choked her with a tight hug.

"There is one small change of plans I was considering," he said. "I hope Dad wouldn't mind."

"What's that?" she asked.

"Instead of the Army, I was thinking Marines."

Tracie responded with "Oh!" Looking at the man on her son's right, it was very clear why he had the change of heart. As far as she was concerned, it was well-earned.

"Your father would not mind at all. He would be extremely proud. Just like I am."

Jon nudged his new friend, Kane Carpenter, with his elbow "They produce some pretty tough guys as well."

Tracie looked at Kane with deep affection and appreciation. "I'd have to agree."

They sat together and watched the ocean, full of admiration for one another.

Check out other great

Sea Monster Novels!

Michael Cole

CREATURE OF LAKE SHADOW

It was supposed to be a simple bank robbery. Quick. Clean. Efficient. It was none of those. With police searching for them across the state, a band of criminals hide out in a desolate cabin on the frozen shore of Lake Shadow. Isolated, shrouded in thick forest, and haunted by a mysterious history, they thought it was the perfect place to hide. Tensions mount as they hear strange noises outside. Slain animals are found in the snow. Before long, they realize something is watching them. Something hungry, violent, and not of this world. In their attempt to escape, they found the Creature of Lake Shadow.

C.J. Waller

PREDATOR X

When deep level oil fracking uncovers a vast subterranean sea, a crack team of cavers and scientists are sent down to investigate. Upon their arrival, they disappear without a trace. A second team, including sedimentologist Dr Megan Stoker, are ordered to seek out Alpha Team and report back their findings. But Alpha team are nowhere to be found – instead, they are faced with something unexpected in the depths. Something ancient. Something huge. Something dangerous. Predator X

Check out other great

Sea Monster Novels!

Michael Cole

MEGALODON VS COLOSSAL SNAKE

Brought to life by the miracle of DNA cloning, a 93-foot Megalodon shark has escaped captivity. With an insatiable appetite and unmatched aggression, it travels west for the Georgia coast, leaving a path of destruction in its wake. Bullets and harpoons can't penetrate it, steel nets can't hold it, and it's only a matter of time before the whole world finds out about it. In a race to stop the beast, the organization responsible recruit a marine biologist and a herpetologist to develop a plan to catch it. To do it, they must unleash the company's other genetically modified experiment—a 150-foot snake, resurrected from the DNA of the mighty Titanoboa. The pursuit leads to inevitable combat, and the scientists are forced to witness the deadly realities of genetic tampering. As the battle escalates, it is clear nobody is safe...and that nature never intended for these beasts to return. As the destruction mounts, and the death toll climbs, the true loser of Megalodon vs. Colossal Snake is humanity.

Tim Waggoner

TEETH OF THE SEA

They glide through dark waters, sleek and silent as death itself. Ancient predators with only two desires – to feed and reproduce. They've traveled to the resort island of Las Dagas to do both, and the guests make tempting meals. The humans are on land, though, out of reach. But the resort's main feature is an intricate canal system . . . . . . and it's starting to rain.

www.ingramcontent.com/pod-product-compliance
Lightning Source LLC
Chambersburg PA
CBHW072237190626
46809CB00018B/2834
9781923165854